Sour Grapes

Lisa R. Schoolcraft

Sour Grapes

Lisa R. Schoolcraft

Table of Contents

Chapter 1

The late March fog enveloped the floor-to-ceiling windows of Laura Lucas's penthouse condo in Buckhead. She felt enclosed, trapped by the gloom.

Laura had recently lost two valuable, wealthy clients. Was it her fault that the wife of her biggest commercial real estate client found out they'd been sleeping together? Laura certainly hadn't blabbed about their affair. That asshole had suddenly developed a conscience and confessed the whole thing to his wife.

Now he wanted to "fix" his marriage. That's what he'd told her when they'd had dinner two nights before. As they left the restaurant, he announced that he was firing her.

The second client, a metro Atlanta high-end residential home builder, said he'd run out of budget before the end of his company's fiscal year. He decided he could have his assistant do public relations and marketing.

Some 22-year-old blonde airhead could never bring in the $200,000 worth of publicity and business she'd garnered over the years for the company. Laura was furious.

Laura needed to find some new clients and needed to find them quickly. Her penthouse mortgage wasn't going to pay itself. She just needed one good client. One wealthy client.

Laura thought about who she knew in town with money and who might need to hire her.

Kyle Quitman recently bought a majority interest in Laura's former lover's company for $3 million. If Quitman had $3 million to buy a majority stake in Marc Linder's LindMark Enterprises Inc., he probably had much more than that.

Given the history between Laura and Marc, she knew Marc would never introduce her to Quitman. And she desperately needed an introduction.

Laura wanted to know if Quitman had a public relations and marketing professional working on his team. If he didn't, she wanted to make sure he hired her for the job. And why wouldn't he need her services? She was good at what she did. She made big things happen for companies.

She began to research everything she could on Black Kat Investors. She discovered it had recently bought a small winery in California – Star 1. That was a curious investment, Laura thought. But if Quitman had money to blow on a winery, why not hire her?

Laura was sure she could work her magic for Black Kat Investors. She'd have to get the number — a personal cell number — for Quitman. She wasn't about to try to go through a receptionist. She'd never get a meeting that way.

Laura was born and grew up in Miami, the granddaughter of Cuban immigrants. The daughter of a businessman and a housewife, Laura had an older brother, Ricardo — Rico — to his friends.

Rico was eight years older than Laura. The oldest son. The golden child. And in her mind, he threw it all away.

"Rico," she muttered. Laura grimaced when she thought of him. He could have had it all. Their father was grooming him to take over his business.

Laura grew up happy. She was the apple of her father's eye and treated just like the annoying kid sister that she was to Rico. Laura adored Rico.

Rico started drinking and smoking in his teens and Laura thought he was so cool, with his slicked back shiny black hair. He had cool friends, wore cool clothes, drove a cool sports car.

Sometimes he'd give Laura a taste of his beer. She winced as she swallowed it and Rico would laugh at her. When she became a teenager, he'd even give her a couple of his cigarettes, but she choked on each one.

As she got older, Laura could see the cracks in Rico's cool demeanor. She realized he had gotten into the drug trade. It made her nervous. For him, for her and her family.

Any time she heard about a gang shooting involving drugs, she stayed up late to make sure Rico came home.

Her worries about Rico never faded, until she met his friend Julio. She fell head over heels for Julio.

He was older than Rico, 10 years older than Laura. On his arm, she felt like a princess. He was kind, he was attentive. When he took her into his bed for the first time — her first time — he was gentle, careful that he didn't hurt her. Until he did hurt her.

"I'm sorry, mariposa, but Rico needs to learn a lesson that he can't cheat us," Julio said, slapping Laura hard. "I'm going to have to break your wings."

Laura's head snapped to the left and she could feel the muscles in her body tense with fear. Her eyes watered and her nose began to run. Her face stung from the slap. Julio slapped her hard again. He hit her so hard she felt faint. Her head swam. She felt blood on her lip where it had split open.

"Why?" she asked him, her eyes pleading for an answer. "Why are you doing this?"

"Shut up!" he shouted, slapping her again, knocking her down to the floor.

Laura hit the floor hard, breaking the heel of her stiletto shoe. "Ah!" she cried out.

Julio reached down and pulled Laura up by her dress, ripping it. "We don't need all of those clothes, now do we?"

"Julio, please don't," she pleaded. "I'm sure Rico…"

But Julio slapped Laura again. She could feel her left eye swelling, and she felt like she might be sick.

"Rico cheated us. He kept the drug money he owes us. He'll learn he can't cheat us. You'll be the one to tell him."

"I'll tell him whatever you want me to," Laura whispered, frightened now. She'd never seen Julio act this way, especially toward her. He was her boyfriend after all. Was. She'd never be able to trust him or look at him again. Or let him touch her again.

Julio's hand grabbed Laura by the throat. She couldn't breathe. She tried to fight him, tried to scratch him. He just slapped her with his left hand while he held her throat. He was so much stronger and bigger than she was.

Laura felt light-headed, like she might pass out. All she could do was mouth the word "stop" but no words came out.

Her vision began to blur, then go black. She passed out and Julio caught her as she crumpled to the floor.

Rico got a message on his pager with a number he didn't recognize. He wasn't fazed. He got messages all the time from numbers he didn't recognize. Mostly likely it was to a pay phone.

Rico called the number to hear a man's voice he didn't recognize that there was a package waiting for him at the usual drop.

Rico drove to the vacant warehouse in an industrial park near the Port of Miami. He drove around the block twice to make sure there were no cops around. When he went in, he found Laura naked, bloodied and unconscious.

He quickly checked for a pulse and was relieved to find her still alive. He looked around and grabbed a dirty drop cloth he found on a metal table nearby. Rico draped it over Laura's body and shook her shoulder gently.

"Chichi," he said, using a term of endearment he hadn't used since they were young children. "Are you alright? Chichi, chichi, speak to me," he pleaded.

Laura stirred, moaning.

"Laura, Laura, wake up," he said. "We've got to get out of here."

Laura moaned again, trying to see through her black eye. "Rico?" she croaked. Her split lip reopened, and blood began to ooze from it.

"Yes, it's me. I'm here. You're safe. Can you sit up? We've got to get you out of here."

"Where am I?" she whispered.

"You're in a warehouse. Do you know how you got here? Do you know who did this to you? I'll kill the bastard who did this to you, Chichi."

Laura tried to move but she hurt everywhere. She hurt between her legs, too. She had a vague thought that she might have been raped. Would Julio do that to her? She was sick at the thought he probably had.

Laura felt betrayed and ashamed when she realized Rico had found her was naked.

"We've got to get out of here. Can you get up or do you want me to carry you?"

Laura put her arm up to get Rico to help her stand. She held the drop cloth tight around her as Rico pulled on her right arm. She limped across the darkened warehouse and squinted at the light when Rico opened the door.

His red Ford Mustang was right outside the door. He opened the passenger door and helped ease her into the bucket seat. Laura looked down and could see blood on her legs.

She tried to wrap the drop cloth around her body as Rico got behind the wheel and started the car.

"Who did this to you?"

"Julio," she whispered. "He said you needed to be taught a lesson. What have you done, Rico?"

Rico couldn't hide the shock on his face when Laura said the name of his friend and her boyfriend.

"Julio did this to you?"

Laura could only nod her head as a tear rolled down her face from her eye that wasn't blackened and swollen. She didn't even want to look at her face in the mirror, but she saw a glimpse in the side mirror.

"I think I should go to the hospital, Rico," she whispered. "I'm hurt."

"No hospitals. They'd only call the police. No police. We can't go to the police. I can't let Mami and Papi see you. You'll have to come back to my place. You can get better there."

"I'm supposed to be at school Monday," she said. She was in her senior year of Catholic high school.

"You'll have to call in sick."

Laura began to cry softly when she realized Rico wasn't going to help her. He was only trying to save his own skin.

Rico unlocked his apartment in an upscale part of Jade Beach and helped Laura into the living room. His high-rise apartment overlooked the beach.

"You can stay here," he said. "I'll go to Mami and Papi's house and get you some clothes for the week. What else do you need?"

"A week? You think I'll be healed in a week? You're crazy. I should be looked at by a doctor. I think I was raped, Rico."

Rico winced at the word "raped."

"I'll fucking kill that bastard," Rico swore. "But no hospitals, Chichi. No cops, either. They'd only ask too many questions."

Laura began crying, pulling the drop cloth tighter around her. She'd been ashamed to be seen by the few people in the lobby who saw her and Rico walk in.

"What do you need, Chichi? I'll get it from your room."

"I need my toothbrush, my comb, my underwear, a couple of bras, and some clothes. What are you going to tell Mami and Papi? What lie are you going to tell them?" she asked, angry now.

"Don't talk to me like that. I'm doing this for your own good."

Laura didn't follow his logic. He was just trying to get out of trouble, and he was going to make it worse.

"I want to take a bath. Do you have a T-shirt and shorts I can wear when I'm done?"

Rico walked back to his bedroom and threw a blue T-shirt and some sweatpants he normally wore to the gym to her. She caught them without dropping the drop cloth around her.

"Here. I won't be gone long, but lock the door and don't let anyone in, Chichi." Rico put his hand on her swollen cheek. "You'll be safe here."

"Will I?" Laura asked as she walked back to the bathroom to take as hot a bath as her skin could stand.

Slowly Laura's body began to heal. She had to wear some foundation to hide the last of her black eye, but she was back in school the next week. She told them she'd had the flu and Rico managed to forge a doctor's note for her. He'd told her parents something similar. That she'd fallen ill at his house and he looked after her. He'd had to convince their mother not to come over to tend to her.

In the end, she realized what an accomplished liar he'd become. A charming liar. But it wasn't the end of his problems with the drug gang he'd crossed. She tried to talk Rico out of going after Julio, but it was to no avail.

Three weeks later, Rico and Julio were dead, trading gunfire in the streets of East Little Havana, where gang activity was common. A notice in the paper put the deaths down as crime activity among gang members. Laura thought it was probably true, but Rico's death destroyed her parents. It destroyed her, too.

After the funeral, in which armed gang members stood guard outside the cemetery, Laura and her parents returned to their home. Laura's mother, Carmela, took to her bed and did not get up for weeks.

Laura too was at a loss. She began to do poorly in school, unable to concentrate, especially a month after the attack when she missed her period. Now she was a good girl in trouble.

She knew she couldn't turn to her parents for help. The shame of her attack would become their shame.

She'd have to find her own way to fix her problem, likely in a back alley where money bought solutions. Rico could not help her now.

She ended up at a clinic at a town nearby for her abortion. She was scared and the nurses and doctor were so clinical. She left without a friend to pick her up. She went back to her parents' house, holing herself up in her bedroom, telling her mother she had a bad menstrual cycle and not coming down for meals for two days.

Her parents were so devastated by Rico's death, they barely noticed her absence.

After she graduated high school in 1991, Laura decided to attend a small private women's college in Virginia.

Her decision came as a surprise to both her parents. Her father didn't want her to go so far away from Miami, but Laura couldn't stay, trapped by her memories.

A degree in communications, with an emphasis in public relations and marketing, allowed her to use her brain and her beauty.

She arrived in Atlanta in 1995 shortly after graduation as the excitement around the 1996 Summer Olympic Games swelled to near fever pitch.

Hired to help hand out Olympic-sponsored merchandise on Atlanta city streets during the Games, Laura found she was good at sales, too.

After 10 years working for others, she decided to become her own boss, focusing on commercial real estate, which was booming in the mid-2000s. Until it wasn't.

The Great Recession had a catastrophic effect on both the residential and commercial real estate markets all around the country, but especially in Atlanta. Laura found those real estate firms cutting their marketing and public relations budgets and taking the marketing in-house.

She struggled to make ends meet for a few years, but always managed to land on her feet.

Laura smiled when she thought how she'd bought her condo in Buckhead at just the right time, when the builder was going broke and was willing to sell it for well below its value. She'd asked her father to help with the loan, the only time other than college, she'd asked him for financial help.

She could probably ask him for another loan to help tide her over now, but she didn't want to do that. She didn't want him to think she couldn't make it on her own.

Laura had read with interest that Marc Linder, her ex-lover, had sold his company to an investor, Black Kat Investors. Kyle Quitman, the man behind Black Kat, intrigued her. What was he like? He obviously had money.

Laura had worked as Linder's publicist and marketer until Ravyn Shaw entered the picture. Ravyn was just doing a profile story on Marc for a magazine. Or so she said. But Laura saw the sparks fly. Soon Marc had fired Laura and hired Ravyn.

Then they became a couple. A couple! That mousy girl. What did she know about keeping Marc satisfied? Laura had known how to keep Marc satisfied. He'd lusted after Laura.

Laura stood up and paced her condo. She loathed Ravyn. Why Marc chose Ravyn over her she'd never understand.

Laura tried to banish Ravyn from her mind. She needed to find another client and fast.

Laura began calling some old clients and working her network to see what businesses might need her services. She got some tips, but two weeks later she'd only met with two old clients and no one had hired her.

She'd gotten a lot of men who said they'd love to hire her, but they didn't need her services right now. She'd made more calls to her network. Nothing.

By early-April Laura was starting to panic. She had some savings, of course, but it wouldn't tide her over for another two months. She had investments, but she didn't want to cash those out. Not if she didn't have to. Those represented her retirement.

At last, she got a call for a small contract. It wasn't much and it would end at the end of April, but it did give her a little breathing room.

Laura worked up several glossy brochures for a small residential real estate company that included some cardstock inserts. She invoiced as quickly as she could and waited for payment.

But she still couldn't get Black Kat Investors out of her mind.

Laura was going stir crazy in her condo. She was usually out and about with clients, having lunch, drinks or dinner. But with little cash on hand, she was staring at the cream walls inside her home.

She sat back on her black and white leather couch and contemplated how she was going to get Kyle Quitman's cell number and work her way into his businesses.

Laura put out a few calls to more of her male colleagues to see if they could help. But she didn't want to push too hard. She didn't want to tip her hand.

Then she reached out to a few female colleagues. Laura didn't have that many female friends. She was really a "man's woman." She had plenty of male friends, very few female ones.

Laura always felt like she could hold her own with the men, but she never let them get too close. Not after what Julio did to her.

Laura shuddered. She didn't like remembering her past. She wanted to look squarely at her future, and that future included what she could do for Kyle Quitman. If only she could talk to him and make her pitch.

Late that night, one of her male colleagues texted her with a phone number.

You didn't get this number from me, the message said.

Laura smiled as she saved the number into her contacts, adding Kyle Quitman's name to the list. She'd have to remember to send her colleague a nice high-end bottle of bourbon for his efforts.

Laura drew a breath and began to write down notes on a legal notepad. She liked to write in longhand. It helped her to think.

She made four bullet points she would discuss with Quitman tomorrow.

- Black Kat Investors needed a marketing and public relations professional to succeed and move to a higher level.
- She had a proven track record of getting results for her clients and could provide testimonials.
- She'd take any project he named and she'd prove her worth.
- If there was any project that was difficult, like Star 1 Winery, she'd prefer that one.

Laura just hoped clients would give her a testimonial. She couldn't ask her last two. A few from a couple of years ago would probably vouch for her.

She also hoped by asking to take on a difficult project, she could deliver.

Laura yawned. It was well past midnight when she finally quit. She turned out the lights to her condo, setting the security alarms as she did so.

The condo building had security — keycard entry, front desk personnel, security cameras — as well. Laura never trusted anything but her own extra security, a separate penthouse elevator, a steel door and a state-of-the-art alarm system.

Laura had a former military friend who had installed it, without building maintenance knowing about it, or the needed permits. Just the way she liked it.

It made her feel safe in her own home. Laura needed to feel safe. It was the only way she could sleep at night without the nightmares starting.

Laura awoke the next morning and ran through her pitch to Kyle Quitman while she was in the shower.

Laura rarely prayed anymore. She felt like God had abandoned her the day of the attack. She could only rely on herself, her wits, her brains, her beauty.

Still, Laura went to the top drawer of her dresser and pulled out an old strand of rosary beads. She began to work each bead through her fingers as she mouthed a prayer to the Virgin Mary.

Laura could almost hear her mother's voice chiding her not to ask God for personal favors. It was a sin. Then she felt like a fraud. She didn't believe anymore and threw the beads back in the drawer, slamming it shut.

She tried to imagine the best time to call Quitman. She hoped he would answer his cellphone. Laura took a deep breath and dialed.

Black Kat Investors CEO Kyle Quitman did not expect to hear a woman's voice on the other end of his cellphone. He also did not expect to listen to a pitch for why he needed this woman as his public relations and marketing representative. And how did she know about Star 1 Winery?

Quitman realized she'd likely heard about it from the press release that hit the newswires a few days ago.

He tried cutting her off. "Laura, is it? Listen, I really don't need…"

"Yes, you do. You have a new investment in a winery that hasn't been doing all that well, until you invested in it."

How did she know that? Kyle wondered. He'd purchased the winery because the owner had run into money trouble. But that wasn't public knowledge.

Quitman began to listen more carefully.

Laura finished her pitch and told him he needed her expertise.

"You need my knowledge and my contacts to make your winery profitable," she said. "And I'm willing to take on Star 1."

"I'm not willing to hire you," he said.

Laura began to interrupt.

"Let me finish, Laura," Quitman said, curtly. "I'm not willing to hire you, but I'm willing to let you prove your worth."

"I'm not giving you my services for free, Mr. Quitman."

"I'm not asking you to," he responded. "I am willing to send you out to Napa and get me some actionable public relations and marketing that amount to real dollars to the winery. I'll give you a cut of what you pull in."

"Sixty-forty," Laura said. "I get the sixty percent."

Quitman laughed. "Like hell. But I admire your moxie. I get sixty percent. It will give you incentive to pull in big numbers. If you can clear at least $100,000 worth of marketing and public relations, I'll hire you. If not, you get your 40 percent and we part ways. Take it or leave it."

"What choice do I have?"

"None, really, if you want to work with me."

"Well, I guess it's a deal then," Laura said, unhappy at this test. Forty thousand dollars wasn't going to get her through two months.

"Deal. Text me your contact information and I'll make the arrangements for you to fly out to California. How much time do you think you'll need?"

"I'm likely going to need three to four weeks to pull in some real dollars. Magazines work on longer deadlines and I'll have to hustle to get the winery into some of them. Newspapers have shorter deadlines, and I might be able to get that done in the first weeks."

"OK, you've got one month to pull this all together. When can you be ready to leave for Napa?"

"I'd need just a few days to clear up some other work for clients," she lied. "Then I'll make Star 1 my top priority."

Laura hung up and knew her work was cut out for her. She'd likely taken on more than she could deliver, but she wouldn't go down without a fight. She turned on her laptop and began to pull every scrap of information she could on Star 1 Winery and the newspapers and magazines in the Napa region.

She needed editor names, reporter names and freelance photographers in the area. She researched wedding magazines that were regional. She sent out several emails and hoped they would land in the right inboxes.

Laura made her pitches as dramatic as she could, considering she hadn't seen the winery yet. If the place turned out to be a dump there wouldn't be much fairy dust, she could sprinkle on it.

Sour Grapes

The winery website didn't mention an event space and she prayed it had one. She could see why Quitman might need her help. The winery sounded pretty lackluster based on its website, which seemed amateur at best.

That was another thing she could probably spruce up. Get some decent copy on the website and begin selling it as a place for a girls' brunch space, a place for a private chef to do a special anniversary dinner or special date night, a bridal shower, a wedding venue. None of that was listed on the anemic website.

Laura drew up a list of things she thought Quitman ought to change on the website right away. She texted her list to him, then she sent him her info. She said she could be ready to fly out in two days after tying up some work for other clients.

Laura didn't need to tie up any loose ends with clients. She didn't have any. But she certainly didn't want Quitman to know that.

She was delighted when she found out she'd be flying out to Napa in mid-May on Quitman's private plane. She almost salivated at the thought of how much money he had. She knew he had a wife, but she hoped that wasn't permanent.

Laura had tried to do some digging but couldn't get any definitive numbers on Quitman's net worth. But a private plane meant he was loaded.

Since she expected to be out in Napa for at least a month, she researched the weather and packed accordingly. She threw in some dresses, light sweaters, skirts, cotton pants and cotton blouses, some sandals and her stiletto heels. She loved how those shoes made her look tall and feel sexy.

As she drove to the DeKalb-Peachtree Airport, which catered to Atlanta's private planes and corporate aircraft, she could have sworn she saw Marc Linder's girlfriend, Ravyn Shaw, driving the opposite way.

Laura pulled over to the terminal where she'd been directed and parked.

Was Marc going to be on this trip to the winery? Well now, Laura thought, this trip just got very interesting.

Chapter 2

The pilot came out to greet Marc Linder, former CEO of LindMark Enterprises Inc., taking his bag. "I'm Ryan Hays. I'm your captain on today's flight," the pilot said, introducing himself. "No flight attendant today."

"That's fine," Marc said, surprised at Ryan's young age. Was he even old enough to fly the plane? he wondered.

"But there's snacks back in the cabin, so help yourself. There's a fully stocked bar, too."

"Even better."

"We're just waiting on my co-pilot and one more passenger," the pilot said.

"Oh, no," Marc replied. "My fiancée couldn't make it."

"No, there's another woman coming. Kyle said so."

Marc was confused. Who else was coming on the trip? He looked over and saw Laura Lucas walking from one of the terminals at DeKalb-Peachtree Airport, commonly called PDK.

"Laura," Marc said under his breath. He said it almost as a swear.

Laura Lucas and Marc went way back. Back to his days when he was running LindMark Enterprises. He'd hired Laura to be his public relations representative. At first, she'd kept their relationship very professional.

Then Laura had made her move on Marc. The next thing he knew they were sexual partners. And Laura liked to amp up their sexual encounters. They had sex behind a nightclub; in Piedmont Park; in a dark alley behind the High Museum; on a hiking trail in Stone Mountain.

Laura liked the thrill of public sex and nearly being caught. Marc got swept away by her dangerous nature. He could feel himself getting hard just thinking about that earlier time.

"Hello, lover," Laura said with a sly smile as she approached him. "Where's your girlfriend? Did she ditch you already?"

"My fiancée, Laura," Marc said. "She couldn't make the trip."

"You're engaged? I'm surprised. Can't believe you'd want to be tied to that little mouse for an eternity. I hope you've got a divorce attorney on speed dial."

"Laura," Marc growled.

"And she's not here? That's too bad for her and good for me," Laura purred.

"Why are you even here?"

"Didn't Kyle tell you? I'm his new public relations representative."

"He did not tell me," Marc said. "I'm not happy about it."

"You don't have to be happy about it. I'm his new hire and I'm going out to help get some publicity for this little rinky dink winery. I'm going to get him some valuable dollars and cents and results. Why are you going out?"

"I'm going to look over the operations. Make sure they are in order and running well."

"Well, give me a hand up, Marc," Laura said, extending her hand as she stepped on the stairs into the plane, an eight-passenger Cessna Citation.

Marc took Laura's hand and could immediately feel a spark between them. He was not looking forward to the flight. He planned to head to the well-stocked bar as soon as he could.

Marc was pleasantly surprised to find high-end liquor aboard Black Kat Investors' private jet. Marc drank scotch, a nice single malt, almost the entire flight. Laura sat across from him in the jet sipping white wine. Her short skirt riding up so he could see her smooth legs. He tried not to think about the time those legs were wrapped around his neck.

Laura asked him if he was staying at the B&B Quitman had suggested. He nodded. "Oh, that's great. I am, too. We can have dinner together," she said.

Marc shook his head no. He didn't want to be around Laura. He was only too familiar with her whiles and whims. He wasn't going to fall for that again.

"Oh, come on," Laura said. "You're not afraid to have dinner with me, are you? I know you, Marc. You wouldn't be rude to a woman."

"I'm not having dinner with you, Laura. We are not going to be spending time together. I'm sorry if that disappoints you."

"What disappoints me is your commitment to Ravyn. She's a mouse. She won't give you what you want, what you need."

"And you will?"

"Of course, I will," Laura said, coming to sit next to him. "You know I will."

"No, Laura. You can never give me what I want. I want a real woman. A woman who won't play games the way you did. With you it was all a game, a sport. I need stability in my life and Ravyn gives me that."

Laura smiled her knowing smile. "You don't need Ravyn. You need someone exciting like me," she said, her eyes flashing. "You need to feel alive, Marc. You need me."

Laura gave Marc a wicked smile and tried to reach his crotch with her foot. "Want to join the mile-high club?"

"No, Laura," he said, batting her foot away. "Not with you."

"Too bad. I know Ravyn wouldn't even suggest doing that. She's a mouse. A little timid mouse."

Laura made little squeaking noises.

Marc wouldn't even dignify Laura with an answer. He spent the rest of the flight in silence, drinking scotch. He felt slightly buzzed by the time they landed, nearly five hours later.

"Can you help me with my bags, Marc?" Laura asked after they landed. "And we'll share an Uber."

Laura hadn't even asked. It was a statement. Like she and Marc were going to spend the long weekend together. Like she was running the show. He didn't want it this way. But she was right. It wasn't in him to be rude to her. And he hated that about himself.

They exited the terminal at Napa County Airport and Laura turned to Marc to get the Uber. He was irritated that she expected him to do everything for her, but he did and at last the Uber SUV arrived to take them to their B&B.

Laura settled into the back seat, but Marc sat sullen.

Laura leaned up to the Uber driver. "Can you recommend a good restaurant for dinner tonight?"

"I recommend Celadon," the driver said. "There is a nice patio and the weather is supposed to be excellent tonight."

"What kind of food is it?" Marc asked.

"Well, it's American, but it's really good," the driver said.

"Let's go there," Laura said. "Do we need to make reservations?"

"You probably should," the driver said.

Laura pulled out her cellphone and began searching for the restaurant. She punched at her phone and then announced to Marc they had reservations at 6 p.m. "I made the reservations early since I knew you'd be tired and on Eastern time, and you've been drinking."

Marc scowled at her. It was none of her business if he'd been drinking on the plane. Why was she assuming he'd be tired? Even though he knew he would probably be.

"I'll be fine," he said, blankly. "I just want to get to the B&B and freshen up."

"Need some help freshening up?" Laura asked, coyly, placing her hand on Marc's arm.

Marc jerked his arm away. "Not from you, I don't."

Laura smiled knowingly. With Marc's girlfriend Ravyn out of the picture this weekend, she was determined to get Marc into her bed.

Chapter 3

Marc and Laura met Robert Pierce Saturday morning for a tour of the winery. He planned to show them the grounds, explain the art of winemaking, before showing Marc the records he kept of the winery.

Laura realized she'd be on her own after the tour. But she'd spied some shops on the way to the restaurant last night, so she'd be able to keep herself occupied.

"Mr. Pierce, thanks for meeting with us this morning," Marc said, shaking Robert's hand.

"Please, it's Bobby. Mr. Pierce is my late father."

"Well, I'm Marc and this is Laura,"

Bobby rolled his eyes as he looked down at their feet. "Did you bring any old boots or shoes you don't mind getting dirty?"

Laura laughed. "You're kidding, right?"

She dressed as she would to meet any client, a rust-colored blouse cut very low, showing off her ample cleavage, and her leopard print short skirt. She was also wearing leopard print Jimmy Choo stiletto heels, giving some height to her petite frame.

Bobby gritted his teeth. He really didn't want Marc or Laura there. But Kyle Quitman was the new boss, so he was going to have to babysit these two, giving them a tour. He could tell they were two city slickers. No idea about a winery and what it took to run one.

"This is a working farm, essentially," Bobby explained, patiently. "We don't have cows or pigs, but we do have tractors and other farm equipment. It can get pretty dusty when it's dry and muddy when it's wet. We've had rain recently, so the ground is probably muddy. Let me see if I've got some spare boots for the both of you. Might be harder to find some for you, Laura. I have mostly men's boots."

Laura just frowned. "That's fine. I'll make do."

Bobby returned from a shed with two pairs of large boots. He handed one pair to Marc and the other to Laura. "You might want to take those heels off and just wear these without any shoes on."

Laura made a face and tried to put her stilettos in the first boot, then the second. She tried walking and immediately fell over. Bobby caught her under her arms as she went sideways. His hands touched soft round flesh.

Laura smirked as Bobby blushed, dropping his hands as Laura righted herself. She then sat on a nearby bench and removed both boots, then her shoes, reluctantly putting her bare feet in the boots. "I hope I don't get athlete's foot from these!"

The boots were too large for her, but Laura wasn't going to be left behind on the tour.

"Let's start out in the ATV to get out to the far end of the vineyards. We can walk around when we get there, and I'll explain a bit about how we grow the grapes and the process of winemaking."

Bobby hopped in the driver's seat while Marc gave Laura a hand up into the passenger's seat before he climbed in the back.

Bobby drove slowly for about 40 minutes, starting and stopping occasionally, talking about the grapes grown, what they were used for, the equipment they used to irrigate the vines when the winery didn't get enough rain. They could see low fencing around the perimeter of the vineyard.

He explained 2015 was turning out to be a dry year, so irrigation lines were necessary to keep the vines on track for harvest.

The vines had budded in March and had bloomed earlier in May, but it hadn't rained much. They'd gotten some rain two nights before, which was welcome.

"Are you worried?" Marc asked.

"I'm always worried about my vines," he replied.

When they arrived at their destination, Bobby hopped down and walked around to help Laura, who had already started to get out of the ATV. She slipped and put her hand out to catch herself, but her right boot was stuck fast in the mud and now her hand was filthy, too.

"I'm stuck!" she exclaimed.

"Let me help you," Bobby said. "Hold onto my arm and pull your leg up. Your boot might stay in the mud, but I'll get it out."

Laura pulled her foot as best she could, but her boot remained in the ground. At least her foot was free. She clung to Bobby so she didn't fall back in the mud.

Laura could smell his musky sweat and the faint scent of his soap. She noticed the eagle tattoo on his arm, just under his T-shirt sleeve, and the full tattoo sleeve on his opposite arm.

"Nice ink," she commented.

Bobby smiled shyly. "Got them after my father died. He wouldn't let us boys get any sort of tattoos when we were younger. Said those were for motorcycle gangs. Once he was gone I could do as I pleased."

Laura could sense Bobby's displeasure at her being there, but she felt herself get a little aroused by the moment. Maybe this trip wasn't going to be so bad after all.

Bobby put the ATV in the storage garage as Laura came around the corner.

"Hey there," she called out.

"Hey yourself. Just put those boots back on the bench," Bobby said, shaking his head toward the rear of the shed.

"Thanks for the tour," Laura said. "Although I thought I'd see grapes out there. This is a winery."

"Not yet. Too early in the season."

"A lot of what you said about wine making was over my head. I just like to drink it."

"I'm here to help. Just a tour guide for Kyle's guests," Bobby spat.

"You don't seem happy that Marc and I are here."

Bobby rounded on Laura. "I'm not. I don't like you or Marc here getting into my business."

Laura was shocked at Bobby's anger but tried to keep calm. "Well, you did sell the place to Black Kat. What did you expect? Kyle's going to want to make some changes."

"Fuck that. Star 1 was running just fine before the sale."

"Sounds like you didn't want to sell," Laura said.

"I didn't," Bobby said, wiping his dirty hands on an even dirtier rag.

"So why did you sell then?" she asked.

"I had to."

"Had to? I don't see anyone holding a gun to your head."

"The bank did," Bobby frowned.

"Ah," Laura said. "The bank."

"The bank," Bobby said, like it was a swear word.

"So, a lot of debt on the place?"

"Yes, but what would you know about that, Miss Jimmy Choos?"

"Well, you know stylish shoes."

"I know stylish shoes. My wife – my ex-wife – spent a lot on her clothes and shoes. Just like you."

"Is that why you are in debt?" Laura asked. "Your ex-wife?"

"Back off, lady. You aren't my divorce lawyer or my banker."

Laura put her hands up in surrender. "Sorry. Just trying to make conversation. I'm not here to argue with you or get into your business, as you say. I'm here to get some publicity and events – you know, money – into this place."

"And you can just wave your magic wand and make that happen?" Bobby said with a sneer. "Kyle's just sent his spies to look in on me. Is that it?"

"Listen, you don't have to be snippy with me. I'm good at what I do."

"I just bet you are," Bobby said, coming closer to Laura, who was a good head shorter than he was. He towered over her. "I know all about women like you."

"Women like me?" Laura said, angrily.

"Yes, women like you. Think you know everything. How to run everything. This isn't some toy you can play with. This is a winery. It's a delicate operation. We pray for sun and just enough rain every year and then pray the grapes grow into fat sugar balls that we can harvest into good wine."

"And why can't a woman like me get some events in here, get some publicity for the winery?" Laura said, truly angry now. She placed her hands on her hips and looked up into Bobby's face. "You're just a misogynist. You wish women had stayed barefoot and pregnant, instead of being able to run circles around this winery."

Bobby burst out laughing. "Misogynist? That's a big word for such a little girl like you."

Laura squinted her eyes at Bobby, almost a foot taller than she was, wishing she could strike him dead. "Fuck you, Bobby."

Bobby had grabbed Laura's arms pinning them to her body. "Don't say things you don't mean, Laura."

"Don't you put your goddamn hands on me ever again," she spat.

"Don't worry, I won't." He released her arms, pushing her back from him and walking out of the shed.

Marc had been so busy since he'd arrived at the winery, he hadn't called Ravyn. He got a text from her during that night's dinner with Laura Lucas.

Sorry I haven't called yet. The operations and books here are in a bit of a mess. At dinner now. Can I call you later?

Honey, the girls have worn me out again. And I've had lots of wine. I'm going to bed. Talk to you tomorrow then. Love you.

Love you, too.

Marc looked up from his phone at Laura Lucas. She'd insisted they try a different restaurant tonight. After all, she'd said, this was a business expense.

"Does the mouse miss you?"

"Stop it, Laura."

"Why isn't she here again?"

"I already told you. Her friend is in the hospital for surgery and needed help looking after her children."

"Ugh!" Laura said, shaking her shoulders, as if the thought of children was revolting. "I never want kids. Snotty, germ-filled rug rats."

"That's why we'd never be a couple, Laura. I want children."

"You? I figured you for the bachelor playboy. I don't see you as a father."

"Why not?"

"You never said a kind word about your own father when we were together. You always complained about him. How much you disappointed him when you gave up your career as an attorney."

"That's not true," Marc protested. "I may not have gotten along with my father at times, but I still respect him."

"Respect him, yes, but can you say you love him?" Laura asked, pointedly.

Marc started to protest again, but then stopped. He wasn't sure he could say he loved his father. Marc's father was a hard man to love, in Marc's opinion. Edward Linder hadn't made loving him easy.

"What are you ordering?" Marc asked.

"You're changing the subject."

"Maybe I am. Just drop it, Laura."

"OK, so I'm thinking about the mussels. And I'd get a white to go with that."

"So, I need to get either seafood or chicken to share your white."

"No, you get what you want. We can always bring the wine back to the B&B and finish it there."

"Hmm, a steak sounds good. And they have a really good Cab here."

"Well, get that and we can just bring the bottles back with us, unless we finish the bottles here."

"I'm not sure I'm drinking an entire bottle of Cabernet here," Marc said.

"You never know. You might enjoy the evening more than you expect. Besides, we're taking an Uber back."

Laura and Marc downloaded into small talk, then stopped talking all together when the food arrived. Marc wasn't comfortable around Laura anymore. He felt like he always needed to keep his guard up.

For her part, Laura sat in silence trying to figure out how to seduce Marc. It wasn't that she was all that attracted to him anymore. His millions made him more attractive. But it just burned her ass that Marc had proposed to Ravyn. Ravyn! That goodie two shoes. Marc was definitely settling, in her opinion.

Hell, Laura thought the guy that operated Star 1 was a better sexual prospect. Bobby Pierce was definitely good looking, with that eagle tattoo on his upper arm and another arm with a full tattoo sleeve. It had roses, skulls and more that she'd like to run her fingers over. And his neatly trimmed goatee. She wondered what that would feel like between her thighs. She gave a little shudder of delight at the thought.

"Everything OK?" Marc asked.

"Huh?" she blinked. Marc's question pulled Laura from her reverie. First things first. Her sights were set on Marc. She'd think about Bobby later.

Marc and Laura ended up finishing their bottles of wine and sharing an Uber back to their B&B. Laura attempted to invite Marc in for a nightcap.

"Nightcap? Are you pilfering the sherry at this place?"

"No. I got a bottle of the scotch you like today while shopping. The Macallan, 12-year, right? Come in and have a nightcap with me."

"I can't. I've got to get up early and work out why those books don't look quite right tomorrow. Bobby's got a good head for business, but I don't understand some of the numbers. The wine was enough tonight."

"Come on, one won't hurt."

"No thanks, Laura. Good night."

Laura shut her bedroom door and brooded. This was going to be more difficult than she thought.

Chapter 4

Despite his objections, Marc and Laura had dinner together every night of their trip, always at a different restaurant in Napa. On the final night, Bobby Pierce wanted to show off the event space he'd created, hosting a dinner with a private chef and some special vintages, including a Cabernet Sauvignon.

"Now this is a space I can work with," Laura said as she saw the setup. "Why didn't Bobby show me this first? I mean I'm trying to get some good PR for this place, and he hides this gem from me."

"Didn't we see this on the tour? It had equipment stored in here, didn't it?"

Marc expressed sympathy, but he had his own worries about Star 1. It wasn't a poor investment for Black Kat Investors, per se, but wine production was likely going to be low this year and some of the vines had been infected with a bacterium. Most of the vines could be treated, others would have to be replanted entirely.

Marc would write up a report tomorrow on the flight back to Atlanta. He knew Quitman had done his due diligence before the purchase. Given some of the problems he'd discovered, Marc was puzzled why Black Kat Investors hadn't uncovered the issues he'd found.

Bobby seemed knowledgeable about how to run the winery. And some of the issues were out of his control. But Star 1 was going to need more capital, in Marc's opinion. He wasn't sure Black Kat was ready for that.

Laura was seated next to Marc at dinner. "So, you're leaving tomorrow?" she asked.

"Aren't you?"

"No. I'm here for about a month. I want to see if I can get a photographer here to shoot this space, see if I can get some publicity in wedding magazines. This place would be perfect for weddings, bachelorette parties, baby showers. I need to hire some models, too. Need to get all that set up, like yesterday."

Marc couldn't suppress his grin and relief. He wouldn't have to fly back with Laura.

"Well, you don't have to look so happy about it," she snapped.

"Oh, Laura, I'm not going to lie and say my flight home won't be a pleasure without you. It will."

"Let's just try to be civil and enjoy the evening tonight," Laura said, forcing a smile and pouring him another glass of wine.

Marc thought she looked like the cat who was about to catch the canary. He suddenly felt like he'd sprouted a tiny beak and little yellow feathers.

Marc and Laura walked up the stairs of the bed and breakfast, Laura carrying a full bottle of wine and two stemmed wine glasses.

She'd cornered a male server in the supply closet, giving him a quick blow job and liberating the special vintage of Cabernet Sauvignon Bobby had served at the party. The glasses she grabbed off the bar.

"Planning to meet someone tonight? Did you invite a waiter from the party?" Marc said, not unkindly.

"No, silly, I'm inviting myself into your room for a nightcap."

"No, Laura. I've had enough to drink tonight and so have you."

"Keeping track of how much I drink? How very sweet of you."

Marc opened the door to his room and Laura pushed her way in. "Come on. Just one drink. I don't want to finish the bottle alone. Then I'll leave. I promise. And you shall remain unsullied and chaste."

"You promise?" he asked, raising an eyebrow. He threw his key card on the table by the TV.

"Scout's honor," Laura said, raising two fingers.

"That's three fingers for Scout's honor, Laura."

"It is? How do you know? Were you the good little Boy Scout?"

"I was."

"I didn't know that about you, but I can see it." Laura placed the wine glasses on the small bistro table in the corner of the bedroom and poured the rich Cabernet she'd nabbed from the server. She still saw the look of sweaty bliss on his face after the blow job. The kitchen staff wasn't getting this bottle for their clean up meal tonight.

A little over an hour later, the bottle was empty.

"Laura, you said you'd leave without a fuss," Marc said.

"I don't think I said I'd go without a fuss, but I will go," she said. She stood up and leaned into Marc and kissed him. He didn't intend to, but he ended up kissing her back. Then he pulled away.

"Laura, you can see yourself out," he said, standing and heading to the bathroom.

Laura turned and as Marc's back was to her, she swiped the key card to his room. "I'll leave, Marc," she whispered. "But I'll be back."

Marc splashed cold water on his face and looked in the mirror. He shook his head and tried not to think about Laura's kiss. He needed to get Laura out of his mind and out of his life forever.

He stripped down to his boxers and got into bed. He opened the window near the bed and felt a cool breeze. After all the wine he'd had that evening, he fell asleep quickly and deeply.

Laura sat in her darkened bedroom wearing her sheer black lingerie. She was waiting until she could be sure Marc would be asleep. His key card felt hot in her hand.

Laura looked down at her phone. The time read 2 a.m. She quietly went to her door and slipped out of her bedroom, heading to his room.

She paused to listen at the door and heard nothing. She really didn't want to be caught by anyone in the hallway, or by him when she opened his door.

She used her phone screen to light the key card lock and slipped it in. Laura heard the click and held her breath. She slowly opened a door and slipped into Marc's room.

She used the dim light of her phone's screen to light her way and felt a chill from the open window. Goose flesh rose on her skin and her nipples became erect.

Laura smiled. That would help in her quest. She peered into the darkness and spotted Marc's phone at the bedside table near him. She walked around the bed and got it.

But she didn't know Marc's password. What could it be? she wondered. She carefully typed in the numeric numbers for RAVYN and it unlocked. Laura smirked at how easy it was to guess his password.

"Jackass," she said under her breath.

She needed to be so careful, but she remembered Marc was a sound sleeper. Laura got his phone and returned to the empty side of the bed. Did she dare to slip into the bed and take the photo? She decided to chance at least sitting on the edge of the bed.

Laura pulled down one strap of her lingerie, exposing her left breast. She licked her fingers and gave her nipple a little tug, making sure it was erect. She wasn't sure it would be visible in the darkened bedroom.

Laura turned her phone camera to take a photo, unable to see if she was getting Marc and herself in the photo, but she stuck her chest out. Snap went the phone's camera. Marc stirred and Laura held her breath. She checked the photo and was delighted to see she'd caught herself and Marc in the photo in his bed.

Marc rolled over, almost touching her. She took one more photo, then tiptoed into the bathroom.

Laura used her phone's light to find Ravyn's name in Marc's contacts, punched Ravyn's number into her phone and sent the photo of her and Marc in the bed. "Enjoyed my time with your boyfriend," she texted.

Laura returned Marc's phone to the bedside table, then placed his key card on the table by the TV where she'd found it. She gingerly crept out of his bedroom and smiled a smug smile.

"I hate you, Ravyn," she hissed as she returned to her room. "He was the best thing that ever happened to me. He should have been mine."

Laura woke up, not hungover, but she felt like she had one. Her head hurt. Maybe she did have a hangover. All that red wine the night before, trying to seduce Marc. She was angry she hadn't been able to change Marc's mind to sleep with her.

Now she had to get the real work done for Star 1 Winery. She really needed to show Quitman she should be his public relations and marketing woman. She desperately needed a wealthy client.

She got up, turning on the coffee maker in her B&B room. She'd get breakfast in a little bit. Right now, she needed coffee. She liked it strong. It was all those years of drinking strong Cuban coffee. She put two packets of coffee in the machine and hit start. When it finished brewing, Laura added about three packets of sugar.

Laura showered and put on a new dress she'd purchased at one of the little shops she'd visited. She hoped she could turn in her receipts as business expenses. She'd have to work her magic on this receipt. Maybe when she hired the models for the photo shoot, she could hide the dress receipt as "wardrobe."

She pulled on a pair of stiletto heels. She smirked when she thought of what Bobby Pierce would say when he saw her outfit. Laura was going to have to turn on her charm with him to allow her to set up photo shoots all around the winery.

She wanted some photos set up in the event space as a bridal shower, a wedding, but then she thought some of the wedding shots should be done in the actual winery itself. Bride and groom with wine glasses.

She worked up a list of things she'd need to complete her task. Hiring models was top of the list. But she'd need to know when they could come and when Bobby could make himself scarce and let her do her job.

Laura could almost hear him push back on her ideas. But Laura knew she would win in the end. She always did. He's just a man, she thought, easily manipulated.

Laura found Bobby in the event room, helping to move some tables back into the catering trucks. There were a few half empty bottles of red and white wines from the winery on the bar.

"Hey, don't put everything away. I may need some of that for the photo shoot," she said.

"What photo shoot? And why aren't you headed back to where you came from? Your boyfriend left already."

"He's not my boyfriend and I'm staying until I can get what I was paid to do."

"Which is what, exactly? Because all I've seen you do is fall all over your not-my-boyfriend."

Laura scowled at Bobby. "I'm here to set up some publicity for this winery. Get models in here. I'm thinking we can do bridal and wedding shoots pretty easily. Here. I have a list of things I'd like to do," Laura said, showing him her notes written on a memo pad from the B&B.

Bobby picked up the memo pad, squinting at her handwriting. "What the hell is this? I can't even read this scrawl."

"You didn't tell me you couldn't read," she said, snatching the memo pad from his hand.

"Hey! I didn't say I can't read. I can't read your writing. It's so tiny. It looks like chicken scratch."

"Well, it's just some rough ideas. But I want to know when I can get some hired models and a photographer in here. I need to put in some calls, but the sooner the better."

"And then you'll be out of here? Out of my way?"

"I didn't realize I was such a distraction," Laura said, smiling widely at Bobby.

"I'd just like you out of my way."

"You won't even know I'm here."

"I highly doubt that. You are the kind of woman who is seen and wants to be seen."

"Why do you say that?"

"Just look at your get up," he said, looking down at her high heels. "I don't know how you walk in those shoes. If you are going to be walking around this winery, you need a good pair of cowboy boots."

"Know where I can get a pair?"

Bobby arched an eyebrow. Surely, she wasn't serious about getting a pair of cowboy boots for the week or so she would be here. Oh God, he thought, what if she was planning to stay longer?

"You can get them in town. The hardware store sells them."

"Hardware store?" Laura exclaimed. "I can't imagine the hardware store has any stylish boots."

Bobby barked out a laugh. "Stylish? They come in brown or black. You don't need stylish around here," he said, gesturing out through the door. "You need good practical boots."

"Well, can you tell me where I can get something that's a little more than brown or black?"

"Can't help you there," he said, pointing to his well-worn brown boots. "Best pair of boots I've ever owned. Had 'em for years."

Laura looked down at the scuffed up faded leather boots.

"I can see that. I guess I'll have to ask someone back at the B&B. But I can schedule the shoots as I see fit?"

"No, you'll have to run them by me first. I can't have a bunch of amateurs running all over the winery. This is a business, Laura."

"I know it's a business, Bobby. I'm trying to get more business out here. Diverse business. Business that doesn't depend on whether your grapes have a bad year."

"What do you mean about a bad year?"

"Marc told me you're having a bad year, some of the grapes have, what did he say? A fungus? It's not catching is it?"

Bobby scowled. "Goddammit. No, it's not catching. I bet your boyfriend will blab the whole thing to Kyle Quitman and make me look bad. I knew I shouldn't have told him that."

"Hey, Marc isn't out to get you, or make you look bad. Kyle asked him to come here to observe the operation because Marc is a businessman like you. Owned his own company before Kyle bought him out for three million dollars."

"Three million dollars? Shit, I didn't get that much! Well, not after what I owed the bank."

"And what did you owe the bank?"

"That is none of your goddamn business."

"Fair enough, but you really want money to be coming in from different areas. And getting this place in wedding magazines as an idea for a wedding venue, or other special events, can boost your bottom line."

"I suppose I really can't say no. It's not my winery anymore," Bobby said in disgust.

"Well, let me help you. I'll call about a photographer and see when I can get models out here. It's California. How hard can it be?"

But Laura found it was hard to book talent. The few places she found didn't have models the right age for when she wanted them. All off making movies in Hollywood or on bigger photo shoots that paid more, she imagined. She could get some booked in two weeks, but that really extended her stay, and maybe overextended her welcome at the winery. She imagined Bobby would not be pleased.

Laura did find a photographer whose portfolio she liked. She was taking such a gamble. She had so much riding on this project. She needed it to go well, too.

Laura decided to meet with the photographer, Lee Adams, out at the winery the next day to go over his ideas and costs for the shoot. She didn't have a company credit card and she wasn't sure Lee would want to invoice after the fact. He'd likely want his money up front. She knew she would. All that would have to be negotiated.

Lee Adams arrived a little after 11 a.m., sheepishly explaining he'd gotten lost trying to find Star 1.

"I thought I knew just about every small winery up here, but my GPS had trouble finding this one," he said, extending his hand to Laura after he got out of his black pickup truck.

Laura felt the crush of his handshake and looked up into his brown eyes. Lee had a slightly crooked smile and a dimple in his cheek.

"Well, I'm hoping with your services, more people will know about this place," she said. "My job is to put this place on the map, so to speak. Let's go into the event space and talk about what I want and what you can do."

"Let me just grab my camera and light meter. I just want to see what kind of light I may have to work with," he said, reaching back into his truck's camper shell and pulling out his camera bag.

Laura led him through the small lobby and around a few corners to the event space where the dinner had been held just two nights before. She pulled out two metal chairs that had been folded against a wall.

"Here, let me," Lee said, putting down his camera bag and helping Laura unfold the chairs. They put them around a small metal card table that hadn't been stowed away.

Lee picked up his camera bag, placing it on the table then got his camera out. He began looking through the viewfinder and shot off a couple of pictures. "Click, click, click," went the camera.

He then looked down at the digital photos. "Well, there's not much natural light in here. I'll have to light this space up, probably. You want photos in here, right?"

"My idea is to set this space up like it is a wedding reception and a bridal shower. We can get tables and chairs and white tablecloths. Maybe some flowers. And models."

"Models are a dime a dozen in California," Lee said.

"Boy I sure couldn't get any before next week."

"I work with a couple of modeling agencies and I can give you a few recommendations. They probably can come sooner than whoever you called. Do you have an age range?"

"I'd want a younger set, diverse models, too. I want to be able to pitch this place to as many magazines as I can."

"You might want to mix up your couples then, a couple of guys, a couple of gals, you know. This is California. And you might consider an older couple, like a second marriage kind of thing."

"Oh, right. I like this brainstorming. Giving me great ideas. Is there a costume shop nearby that I could rent a wedding dress, or a tuxedo?"

"You might find them in the thrift stores. Although they are 'vintage shops' here. But brides give their dresses for resale. I get a lot of my props from vintage shops."

"I guess I better book the models first, then find the clothes and other props I'll need. Ugh. This is going to take some doing."

"I can help if you need it."

"We'd first better discuss your rate. Otherwise, I'll find a teenage girl and hire her for several days to do the legwork. I don't have a car here, so I might have to do just that."

"You can probably afford me," Lee said. "My rate is $150 an hour."

"That's it? I've hired photographers for more than that in Atlanta," Laura said, shocked.

"Well, this isn't Atlanta. My needs are low. Just need gas in the truck, a little weed now and again, and food for my dog," Lee said.

"No wife or girlfriend to buy for?"

"Nope."

"Smart man. You want something to drink? There are some good wines here. Or I can ask the owner if he has a beer."

"You don't drink beer? There are really great craft beers here."

Laura made a face. "I'm in Napa. I'll drink the wine."

"Suit yourself. I'll take a local beer if you've got it."

Laura ducked out of the room to find Bobby, coming back with a Napa Smith brand IPA beer.

"I hope this is what you wanted. Bobby had some in the mini fridge in his office," she handed the bottle to Lee, holding a chilled white wine bottle in her other hand. She put the bottle down on the table and left to find a wine glass and corkscrew.

Coming back to the room, Lee had the bottle open and had poured her a glass.

"How did you do that? Where'd you find the glass?"

Lee held up what appeared to be a Swiss Army knife. "I've had this since my boyhood days. And it pays to have this handy little tool when I'm out in the middle of nowhere for a shoot. The glass was right over there," he said, pointing to a catering rack with several glasses.

"Oh, thanks." Laura sat down across from Lee, who was eyeing her over his beer bottle.

She looked down to make sure a button hadn't come loose on her blouse. "What?" she asked.

"Nothing. Just wondering what a woman like you from Atlanta is doing out here."

"I'm doing my job. I was hired by the guy that now owns this winery to get it some publicity. An article about the winery will only get me so far. But an article or two or three about this place as an event location will get me in several magazines."

"You know what magazines you are going to get them in?" Lee asked.

"Not really," she admitted. "I researched a few that are here, and I've reached out to some, but I've not really gotten any firm answers about features."

"Laura, may I call you Laura?" he asked.

Laura nodded.

"You need my help more than you know. I work for a lot of magazines and community newspapers in the area. Hire me and I'll get you the contacts you need."

Chapter 5

Laura Lucas spun around in Bobby Pierce's office chair, pleased with herself. She'd negotiated a reduced fee from Lee Adams and would allow him to use the photos as he saw fit on his website.

"Taking over my job now, are you?" said a male voice behind her.

Laura jumped up from the chair and turned to face an angry Bobby. "No, I was just…"

"Don't go near my desk. Don't come in this office. I don't want you prying into my things."

"You should be thanking me. We should be celebrating."

"Thanking you? I'll celebrate when you leave this winery."

"Well, I need to talk to you about that. I've hired a photographer and he's got some connections, but we probably can't begin shooting the models until next week."

"You're going to be here next week, too?"

"I told you I'd be here at least a month. Maybe longer."

"Goddammit, I want you out of here," Bobby shouted.

Laura put her hands on her hips and stood her ground. "I'm not leaving here until my job is done. You can't bully me, Bobby Pierce. I've dealt with people far worse than you," she shouted back.

"Well, just stay out of my way and out of my office!"

"Calm down, cowboy. The sooner I'm done the sooner I'm out of your precious winery. But I'm going to need some kind of office to be able to coordinate the people coming in, the schedules. Can't you move a little desk in here for me? I've got my cell, but I need access to the internet, a desk and a chair. I like your chair."

Bobby took a deep breath, trying to keep the edge out of his voice. "You can't have my chair. I'll find you a small desk. Might be something around here you can use, but it will have to do."

Laura returned the next morning to find a small old wooden desk with two drawers on the side and what appeared to be a small wooden crate turned on its end. She supposed that was Bobby's idea of her chair. She eyed it but didn't even think of sitting on it. It would probably collapse and she'd end up with splinters in her ass.

She made a disgusted face, hurled some curse words and stormed off to find Bobby.

Laura was in jeans, a white cotton blouse and her new boots, which she was growing to love for their comfort. She was glad she'd asked someone at the B&B where she could get some cute ones.

"Where's Bobby?" she barked at a dark-haired worker in jeans, boots and a dirty shirt. It seemed to be a common look for the workers here, she thought. "Who are you?"

"Walker."

"Is that your first name or last name?" Laura snapped.

Walker frowned at Laura. "First name."

"Where is Bobby?"

The man glared at her. "Over there," he said, and pointed in a direction that did not include any person nearby.

"Where's there?"

"Down on the far field. He's working on some broken trellises. He's down there trying to fix them."

"And just how am I supposed to get to the far field?"

"Walk, I guess," the man shrugged, clearly angry at Laura.

Laura fumed and began walking briskly in the direction the worker had pointed. She'd walked about 40 minutes when she spotted Bobby out in the middle of the neatly rowed vineyard with a shield over his face and a blowtorch in his hand working on some pieces of wire on the trellis that he had wrapped around his arm.

"Hey!" she yelled. Bobby didn't move. "HEY!"

Bobby looked up, stopped a blowtorch he'd been using to solder the wire to the trellis and lifted his face shield. "What the hell are you doing out here?"

"What is the meaning of that fucking desk and that fucking crate? Is that some kind of joke to you?"

"Desk?! You're out here because of a desk? Get the hell back to the office. I've got work to do. I've got some trellises that need to be fixed. Now get the hell out!"

"I'm not leaving until you tell me what that fucking desk and crate are all about."

"It's temporary, OK? It's all I could find in the storage shed."

As they argued among the tight rows of grape vines, they both heard a loud squeal coming from an irrigation pipe.

"What's that?" Laura asked.

Bobby threw down the blowtorch he'd been using and ran toward Laura, knocking her to the ground. A burst of high-pressure water began spouting straight up from the joint of an irrigation pipe in the vineyard. Water rained down on both of them, soaking them, turning the dirt around them into mud.

Laura screamed as Bobby tried to cover her with his body. "What are you doing? Get off me!" She tried to push Bobby off, but he was heavy.

Bobby scrambled to his feet. "I'm trying to protect you, you idiot! I wasn't sure where the water was going to come out. That's a high-pressure line!"

Laura's perfectly styled hair was now matted down, and she wiped her wet hair out of her face. As she looked down, she could see her white cotton blouse was practically see through and her nude bra wasn't hiding anything. Bobby looked at her, too.

"Ah," was all he could say as he turned his back on her.

"Give me your shirt," Laura commanded.

"What?"

"Your shirt. I can't walk back like this. Your workers will get a full view of my chest, which I'm sure they'd love. Give me your shirt." She held out her hand.

Bobby pulled off his wet dark blue plaid shirt, turned and handed it to Laura. She wrung out as much water as she could and pulled it on, buttoning a few of the buttons across her chest. Then she looked at him admiringly.

Bobby had on an undershirt, but Laura could see he had muscles across his arms, chest and abs. Tattoos on his chest and arms were on full display, too, through the thin white undershirt material. He was in great shape, Laura saw. She gave a little shudder thinking about what it would be like to hold onto those arms while he made love to her.

"Are you cold?" Bobby asked.

"A little bit. How will you stop the water?"

"I've got to cut the water off at the irrigation valve. Wait here."

Bobby began to run off to the far end of the irrigation lines. A few minutes later the water stopped spewing out of the broken joint.

As he walked back, Laura was standing, her arms crossed over her chest. She was shivering in the cool morning air.

"What happened?"

"I think the joint was rusted and it broke. That's a high-pressure line," he reiterated, pointing back to the line. "We could have been hurt. Well, let's get you back to the house. You'll need some dry clothes. Climb into the ATV."

The pair climbed into the ATV as Bobby started the motor. It backfired, then quit. Bobby tried to start it again, but the engine wouldn't turn over.

"Shit," he said, getting out of the ATV. "I think we're going to have to walk back."

"What? Are you kidding me?"

"Well, you walked down here. Now we're walking back," he said, irritably.

The pair walked back in silence, Bobby walking slightly ahead while Laura trailed behind, fuming.

As they approached the main office, Bobby turned to Laura and steered her toward a small house where he lived on the property. Laura was surprised. She'd seen the small building, but she thought it was an outbuilding, a shack, not a home.

"You live here?" she asked.

"Yep. Ever since my divorce. Wife got our big house and I got the winery and this little place. Mostly built it myself."

Laura stepped through the door. It looked like a typical bachelor house. Clothes were on the floor with beer cans and wine bottles on the tiny kitchen counter.

"Take your clothes off in there," Bobby said, pointing to a room behind a door. "I'll find something dry for you while I put these in the dryer."

"You told me you were married."

"Briefly. What about you?"

"Never. And I like it that way," as she handed over her clothes from behind the door.

"Where are your, ah, underthings?"

"I'll let those hang dry in your bathroom if you don't mind. They are too delicate for your dryer."

"Suit yourself," he said as he tossed her wet clothes in the dryer and put them on high. "So, you never married? I thought you'd have been married and divorced about three times by now. Or maybe you like women?"

"I like men," she said through his bedroom door. "I just don't see a reason to get tangled up with one for very long."

"Is that so?"

"That's so."

"I think you're full of shit, Laura," he said to his partially closed bedroom door.

Laura was shocked by his statement. "I am not full of shit, Bobby," she shouted through the door. "I've had to make my way on my own all my life. I don't want to complicate things with a husband."

She came out of his bedroom wrapped in the multi-colored quilt that had been covering his bed.

"I've got some shorts and a T-shirt if you want."

"This quilt is nice and warm. I'm fine."

"That's my grandmother's quilt."

"Family heirloom?"

"You could say that."

"Would you rather I not wear it?"

"I'd rather you didn't. Let me get you something else."

Bobby strode around Laura and walked into his bedroom, rummaged through his dresser drawers and returned with a sweatshirt that said Star 1 Winery in faded lettering and a pair of men's gym shorts that had seen better days.

"Want some coffee?"

"I was thinking a nice glass of that special Cabernet Sauvignon you have would warm me up nicely, too. But if you only have coffee, that's fine."

"Well, I don't normally drink wine this early in the morning," Bobby said as he reached into a cardboard box on the floor of the kitchen and pulled out a bottle of Star 1's special vintage of the Cabernet Sauvignon. He grabbed a corkscrew off the kitchen counter, gave the cork a twist and they both heard the pop as it came out.

Bobby went over to the cabinets and pulled out two low ball glasses, pouring the dark red liquid in them. He handed one glass to Laura. She took it, then reached out to clink her glass to his.

"To success."

Bobby arched an eyebrow. "Success?"

"Yes, to the success of the photo shoot and the publicity and what that means to Star 1."

"What you really mean is what the success will mean for you and the guy that now owns this place."

"Well, that, too. Listen, I just want this all to go well. The sooner it does, the sooner I'm out of your hair."

"You'll leave after the photo shoot?"

"As soon as the shoot is done, I've got to get it into some magazines."

"That could take forever."

"Not forever. I can do some of that from Atlanta. But I may stay just a little longer to make sure the winery will be featured the way we want."

"You mean the way you want."

"I don't want any bad publicity. And if there are any skeletons in your closet you better tell me now."

"No skeletons."

"No winery owner who has five driving under the influence infractions I should know about?"

"None."

"No drug violations either?"

"Does marijuana count?"

Laura looked at him. "Well, not really in my book. But it's good you don't have DUIs. That's the kind of crap I probably couldn't smooth over."

"When is the photographer supposed to be here?"

"He was out here yesterday looking at the event space. He wants to come back later in the week to see how the lighting is out in the vineyard."

"How much is this going to cost me?"

"Not a dime. I negotiated a deal and I'm going to put the invoices through to Kyle."

"That's the kind of deal I like to hear. As long as it's not coming out of my pocket."

"Now we need to talk about that desk and crate."

"Laura, it's temporary so don't break my balls about it."

"I'm not planning to break, or even touch, your balls, Bobby. I just want a decent chair and desk, or at least a decent chair."

"Why don't you go into town and buy a chair, then. Can you invoice that to Quitman?"

"Well, I can try," she hesitated. She wasn't sure how she'd hide a chair for a temporary office into what she was invoicing for publicity. Her new dress and her cute boots, yes, but a chair? Maybe she'd have the models sit in the chair and she could work it in that way. "But what the hell? It's not like I'm flying home with that chair. It will stay here on the vineyard. You buy it."

"I'm not buying you a chair."

"You're a real asshole, you know that?"

"So I've been told. My ex-wife told me almost daily," Bobby said, rolling his eyes, then looking away.

Laura sighed. She didn't need to feel sorry for this asshole. "Are my clothes dry? I'm really ready to leave."

"Well, don't let me stop you." Bobby went into the small room with the stackable washer and dryer and pulled out Laura's pants and blouse.

"I hope you didn't shrink them."

"I don't see how I could. They were skintight to begin with," he retorted.

Laura disappeared behind the bedroom door and returned dressed. Her bra and underwear were still wet, but she put them on. She came out of the room and threw his borrowed clothes at him.

"Thanks for the visit," Bobby said, catching the sweatshirt, but dropping the shorts. "Don't come again."

Laura wanted to slap him. Instead, she turned on her boot heel and strode out of his front door. "Asshole!"

"Bitch," she heard Bobby say as she left.

Chapter 6

L aura got back to her B&B and fumed at Bobby in her head. The gall of that man!

　　She pulled off her clothes and wet undergarments and started a hot bath. She liked the bathroom in her small suite and the big, jetted garden tub. She wished she had one in her condo. She'd opted for a large walk-in shower, and it had served her well when she was entertaining men. She'd had lots of shower sex in there.

Laura eased herself into the tub and turned on the jets to scrub off the mud and grime of the morning. Fresh towels and washcloths were laid out and she put some lavender bath gel on the washcloth and began scrubbing her legs and arms vigorously. But when she got to her torso and chest, she made soft circles on her breasts and nipples.

She began to get aroused. She daydreamed that Bobby was stroking her body and became aroused even more. She reached her hand down and began stroking between her legs. She imagined Bobby stroking her there.

Laura had been very angry with him but didn't want to admit he also turned her on. But in the privacy of the bathroom, she could let her imagination run wild.

She began stroking herself harder with her right hand moving the washcloth over her nipples with her left hand.

Laura moaned with pleasure. "Bobby, Bobby," she whispered. "Fuck me, Bobby. Fuck me hard."

Laura bucked her back with her orgasm, settling back in the warm water, taking a deep breath, feeling blissful. She was a little sorry she'd forgotten to bring her vibrator on this trip, although it wasn't waterproof.

As the water began to cool, Laura got out of the tub and reached for a plush white robe. There were even some white slippers. This B&B had some lovely perks. She put those on and padded out to the bedroom, flopping back on the bed. Before she knew it, she'd fallen asleep.

Laura woke up to darkness. She felt disoriented. And she felt hungry. She obviously slept through lunch and dinner. She was unsure she could find an all-night diner.

She got dressed in a blouse and skirt, grabbing a sweater, too. The nights in Napa in early June were far chillier than early June in Atlanta. She texted for an Uber. Maybe the driver would know where she could eat.

She stood outside the street waiting for a white Acura TLX with a driver named Greg K.

When the driver pulled up, she made sure it was him and climbed into the passenger's side. She never got in the back seat. She felt that was a recipe for disaster.

"Hey, Greg K. What is your real name?"

Greg hesitates for a moment, then replied, "Greg Kincaid."

"Well, Greg Kincaid, I missed dinner at the B&B here, so is there a late-night diner or a restaurant still open nearby?"

"I know a couple of places that are still open."

"Well, take me to one of them. I'm hungry. I want a place I can sit down and order food."

"OK."

They drove for about 10 minutes and Greg pulled up in front of an Italian restaurant.

"Will this do?" he asked.

"Oh, Italian will be great. Greg, what is your phone number? I want you to pick me up after my meal."

Greg gave Laura his cell number and then drove off.

Laura walked into the restaurant, which had a dark interior and a long oak bar.

She walked up to the bar and sat on a bar stool.

The bartender came over and laid a menu down in front of her and grabbed a glass of water, a napkin and place setting and put that down in front of her.

Laura opened the menu and decided on a glass of Chianti and the eggplant Parmesan. She also ordered a Caesar salad.

The salad and wine came first. Laura sipped her Chianti first, then started in on her salad. By the time her eggplant arrived, her first glass of wine was finished and she ordered another.

She finished her dinner and decided to indulge and order dessert. She ordered chocolate torte and then ordered a decaf cappuccino. She felt slightly buzzed, but she wasn't driving.

When she was finished with her meal, she texted Greg and waited outside the restaurant for her Uber ride. The white Acura pulled up and she got in the passenger seat.

"Hello, Greg."

"Hello, Miss Lucas."

"Oh, please, call me Laura."

"Laura. You are my last customer of the night."

"Oh, really?"

There was silence in the car until Greg pulled into the driveway of the B&B.

"Are you off for the rest of the evening?" Laura asked.

"Yes," he replied.

"Are you married?"

"Yes."

"How old are you?"

"Old enough."

"Old enough for what?"

"For what we're about to do."

Laura hesitated. Greg looked like he might be in college. She didn't want to think she could probably be his mother. She turned to him in the dark of the car.

"Would you like to come up to my room for a night cap?"

"Yes."

Laura led Greg up to her room in the B&B. They entered her bedroom and Laura grabbed two glasses from her nightstand and also grabbed a bottle of wine from Star 1. She was glad she'd pilfered a couple of bottles two days before. She wanted a good night cap at the B&B, too.

"I hope you like red wine."

"That's fine. I like whatever you have. You are a very beautiful woman, Laura."

"I'm glad you think so," she said, raising the wine glass to her lips. She kept looking at Greg. He had dark hair and eyes. He was neatly dressed in a white polo shirt and khaki pants.

Greg took a long drink of his red wine and reached out his glass for more. Laura refilled his glass then sat on her bed. "Would you like to sit down?"

Greg sat down next to Laura. "You are so beautiful," he said again. He began to caress her shoulder, then play with her thick black hair.

"You said that."

Greg cupped the back of Laura's neck and leaned in to kiss her. Laura didn't back away. She quickly leaned into him and pulled him down on the bed and its bedspread.

Greg rolled on top of Laura and she reached for his pants, trying to work them off. Greg rolled onto his back, unzipped his pants and pulled them off, then rolled over onto Laura. He reached under her skirt and pulled her panties down to her knees.

Laura shimmied them to her ankles, then kicked them off. She then reached for Greg's penis and began to work her hand up and down until he got hard.

"Let's get under the covers," she said. "I don't want to explain your jacking off on this bedspread."

Greg groaned as he pulled away the bedspread and the sheets. His hard on remained, however.

Laura laid on the soft sheets, as Greg spread Laura's legs apart, then eased himself into her. He began to thrust into her, with Laura moaning with each thrust.

"Deeper, Greg," she said. "Give it to me harder. Harder, baby, harder. Oh God."

"Oh, baby, baby. I'm going to squirt," he said, his eyes shut tight. "I'm going to squirt."

"What?" Laura asked, opening her eyes and looking at Greg's contorted face. "You're going to what?"

"I'm going to squirt. Oh God, I'm squirting."

In what seemed like just a few seconds later, Greg shuddered his climax, then fell on top of Laura.

"Oh God, that was great," he said. "I came hard."

Laura hadn't climaxed and was disappointed. Dammit, she thought. Did he not know what he was doing?

"Well, I didn't cum," she said. "Can you play with my clit? I want to get off."

"What?" Greg asked, confused.

"I didn't cum. Can you help me cum?"

"I don't understand."

"Just because you got off, doesn't mean I did. I need you to help me to get off. Play with my clit. Use your tongue."

"I'm not touching your pussy," Greg said with a look of disgust. "It's filled with my squirt."

Laura pushed Greg off her. "Really? You can't help me get off? No wonder you are willing to cheat on your wife. Probably can't satisfy her either."

Greg scrambled out of the bed, angry.

"How dare you say that!"

"Really? Am I saying anything you don't know? Why are you here with me instead of your wife?"

Greg grabbed his pants and pulled them on, grabbed his underwear, then pulled on his shirt. "I'm out of here, you crazy bitch."

"Good! Get out! You weren't man enough for me!" Laura said through gritted teeth.

Laura had already given Greg a five-star review for the Uber ride. She wished she could give him a one-star review for being a bad lover.

Laura shut the door behind Greg, took off her skirt and blouse and returned to her bed. She was jumpy. The sex had been bad. Really bad. Now she really wished she'd brought her vibrator. She sighed and tried to fall asleep. She began to think of Bobby again as she slowly masturbated.

Laura imagined him naked, with a long hard penis. She'd seen how big his hands were. She imagined the rest of him was just as big. She imagined him entering her. At last, she felt her excitement build, achieving an orgasm. Laura felt her muscles relax, felt a wash of those feel-good hormones flood her body.

"Oh, Bobby," she whispered, rolling over on her side. "I bet you know how to please a woman."

Laura decided she was done with taking Uber rides whenever she had to go out to the winery. She looked up rental car companies and found she could get a rental car for a week and it would come out nearly what she was paying for Uber rides with tips. She called and asked that the rental company pick her up, filled out the paperwork back at their office and got the keys to a compact car.

Laura pulled up to the winery in her white Chevrolet Cruze. She had groaned when she'd stepped on the gas and the car barely sped up. It certainly wasn't her Mercedes, but it would have to do. Her Mercedes was a 4-cylinder too, but at least had Turbo.

"What's this?" Bobby asked as she got out of her rental car.

"I decided I was spending too much on Uber. I needed my own car."

"How long did you rent it for?"

"A week. Then I'll reassess if I'll need it for another week."

"I'm never getting rid of you, am I?"

"Well, not for the next week, you're not. I've got the photographer coming over later today to see the winery in the afternoon light. We've got models lined up for tomorrow, so we're making progress."

Bobby scowled at her. "What about the week after that?"

"Listen, why don't you stop trying to get rid of me. I'm here for more than a week, I expect. Just chill out, Bobby."

"I've got a winery to run and I can't have people tramping all through the vines, getting in the way of my workers."

"Well, I'll let you know when we'll be shooting and try to keep out of your way."

"Do that."

Once again, Laura was furious at Bobby. Why is it every time she spoke with him, they ended up arguing?

"What is your problem?" Laura asked, putting her hands on her hips.

"I don't like you coming in and trying to run things, OK?" Bobby shouted. "You come in here like a princess, with your high heels, low-cut shirts. You are completely out of your element here, but you don't even seem to care. My men are gossiping about you. There's a story you gave one of the caterers a blow job, for God's sake!"

Laura could feel herself flushing. How did they find out about that? Jesus, that kid probably blabbed to everyone.

"Well, you can't believe gossip. They are all just jealous, I suppose. And wishing it was true. Should I start dressing like a school marm? With high-collar dresses and nothing to show but my ankles?"

"That would help. Just stop dressing like you're back in Atlanta. When you go back there you can parade around naked for all I care."

Laura's eyes narrowed. "There is nothing wrong with the way I dress. And I will not be bullied by you, Bobby Pierce. You can shout all you want, but I won't change the way I do things."

"Fine! Just stay the hell out of my way!" Bobby shouted, storming off toward his office.

"Fine! I will!" Laura shouted at his back.

But Laura needed to use the small space for her in Bobby's office, so she followed him in.

"I thought I told you to stay away from me."

"Well, I need to use this office, such as it is. I see you got me an actual chair."

"Yeah, one of the guys found it in another one of the sheds."

"Perfect. I told the photographer Lee Adams to meet me here in about an hour. Until then, I'm going to work on my laptop. What's the Wi-Fi password?"

"StarOne," he said. "The number is spelled out."

"Well, no one would ever guess that password. You'd better change it."

"Bossing me around again?"

"Listen, anyone can guess that password. It's not very strong."

"You didn't guess it."

"Christ! Why is everything so difficult with you?"

"Get off my back. I've got lots of stuff I need to do, too."

Laura walked out of the office to her rental car and got her laptop out of the trunk. She re-entered, opened her laptop, got on the Wi-Fi and didn't say another word to Bobby.

She made several calls on her cellphone to several magazines trying to get features on the winery.

After she'd made four calls, Bobby interrupted her. "Are you going to make more calls?"

"I've got a list of publications I need to call, so, yes."

"Would you mind making them out of the office? I can't hear myself think with you yakking away."

"I have my job to do, too. I'll try to be quieter, so I don't disturb your important work," she said with sarcasm.

Laura walked out of the office and made two more phone calls but had to re-enter the office when she needed to take some notes on her laptop. She unplugged it and walked out again, sitting on a small bench outside with the laptop perched on her knees and her iPhone cradled precariously under her chin.

"I'm sorry, you are breaking up," the woman on the other end of the call said.

"Sorry, I moved outside so I wouldn't disturb the lord of the manor. I must be too far away from the Wi-Fi."

"Lord of the manor?"

"Sorry, the guy who runs the winery. He's a great guy," Laura lied. "But he has work to do in the office and I didn't want to disturb him."

Laura rolled her eyes at what she heard herself say. Bobby was an asshole. But she didn't want Kimberly Gifford, the reporter on the phone, to know that. She wanted Kimberly to think Bobby was great and the event space was great, and all was great.

"Well, I'd love to come out to see the space," the reporter said.

"Sure. How about next week? We've got just a few finishing touches to put on it," Laura said, lying through her teeth. She had no idea how she was going to pull this off.

"Great. How about next Wednesday?"

"That works. Why don't you come shortly after lunch?" Laura didn't want to have to pay for this woman's lunch. She'd get her out in the afternoon, let her see the space, sell her on a feature of the winery and event space and send her on her way.

Laura went back into the office. "Bobby, I need the event space to be up and ready by next Wednesday. I've got a reporter coming to see it and to do a feature."

"What do you want me to do about it? That's all up to you, right?"

"OK. That's fine. I'll take care of everything. But I may need some of your workers to help me move some stuff in and out of the space."

"Just as long as you don't provide any other services to them."

Laura's face darkened. "What do you mean by that?"

"I know you gave the caterer a blow job, Laura. Highly professional."

Laura opened her mouth to speak, then shut it again.

"What? No defense of your actions?"

"Call it a lapse in judgement," she said. "Believe me, it won't happen again. Especially if he's going to blab about it. Jesus, does every man have to talk about getting a blow job? It can't be that rare."

"You're not even embarrassed by your behavior?"

"Why should I be? He got something and I got something."

"What did you get?"

"A great bottle of your Cabernet. One of that special vintages you had at the party."

"Seriously? You could have just bought a bottle."

"Well, in hindsight, I guess I should have just bought the fucking bottle. I'll be sure to do that next time."

"There won't be a next time, Laura. You are NOT to touch any of the hired help."

"Believe me, I won't."

Lee Adams arrived later that afternoon, pulling up next to Laura's car and texting her that he'd arrived.

Laura walked out of the office to meet his truck. Lee stood at the back removing his camera bag.

"Hey there!" Laura called out.

"Hey! Where do you want me to set up?"

"I thought we'd take the ATV out to some of the fields. You might get some great shots."

"OK, great."

"Let me just make sure the boss man will let me borrow the ATV."

"Oh, if it's a problem, we can just walk. I've been driving all over today. I wouldn't mind a walk."

"Oh, OK. That's fine. It might be a bit of a walk, but then you can see what there is."

Laura popped into the office to tell Bobby she and the photographer would be walking the property and they'd be back in a while.

Lee hefted his camera bag over his shoulder and the pair began to walk down the path that led into the vineyards.

Laura was glad she had her boots on. Lee had on athletic shoes. They walked in silence for just a moment.

"Wow. There's not much change to the scenery," Lee said.

"Well, it is a winery. Lots of vines."

"Can we go into some of the rows?"

"I guess that's alright. Just don't drop anything on the vines. Bobby would have my head."

"I'll be careful," Lee said as he moved between the rows of vines. "Hey, are you willing to be my model for this afternoon?"

"Sure, I guess. What do you need me to do?"

"Sit down there," Lee said, pointing to a spot between the narrow vine rows. He raised his camera and shot off a few photos, then looked at the digital shots at the back of the camera.

Laura had sat down, but wished she'd brought a towel or something to sit on. Still, she started to smile as she looked at Lee.

"No, don't smile. I want you to look more natural. Not smiling."

Lee pulled out his light meter and checked his camera's settings.

"OK, turn toward me," he said.

Laura turned her face to the sunshine and Lee shot a series of photos rapidly.

"Now look to your left," he said, "kind of across your shoulder."

Laura turned her body and then looked over her shoulder. Lee shot some more photos.

"This afternoon light is wonderful, Laura," Lee said, looking at the photos he'd shot. "You are a very photogenic woman. Really, you are a natural in front of the camera. Most people look stiff. You're not. Have you ever thought about modeling?"

"Oh, no. I'm a businesswoman, not a model," she said, although she knew she could rely on her looks.

"Well, you sure could be. Let me know if you'd like to do some modeling shots. I'd love to do them for you. No charge."

"Well, I can always use a new head shot."

"I can do that too, but I mean like a model. I'd pose you. Why don't we go out later this week and just shoot a few?"

"But I don't have any modeling clothes. I didn't bring any really stylish dresses or anything."

"Just wear a nice blouse and jeans. It will just be practice."

"OK. If it's just practice."

Chapter 7

Laura returned to her B&B that evening exhausted by all the calls she had been making, all the appointments she'd made, and the several hours she'd spent with Lee out in the winery.

When she entered her room, she saw there was a message on the landline phone. She called down to the reception desk to get the message.

"Ah, yes, Miss Lucas. We have you checking out on Friday. We hope you've enjoyed your stay," the front desk manager said.

"Oh, I'm going to need the room for another week, at least," Laura said.

"I'm sorry, Miss Lucas. We have other guests checking into that room on Saturday. But if you need other accommodations, I'd be happy to help you find a nearby hotel."

Laura was silent. Now that she'd been at the B&B, she didn't want to move to a Holiday Inn.

"Oh, well, let me see what I can find first."

"Very good. But I'm happy to help if you need other accommodations," the manager said.

Laura hung up and frowned. She was enjoying her stay and didn't want to leave. Where would she go? How much was a hotel going to cost? A good one would cost her a lot, even if she did use some of her hotel loyalty points. But what if she couldn't find a Hilton, Marriott or Starwood property? What then?

If she couldn't expense the hotel to Black Kat Investors, it would come out of her commission. She groaned thinking she was not going to make any money for this job.

Laura sat on the edge of her bed, taking off her boots. She debated getting back in the jetted tub. Might as well enjoy it while she could. She ran the water, putting some lavender bath oil in and undressed. She stepped into the warm water and could feel jets begin to ease the tension from her body.

Once again, she moved the washcloth over her body, feeling sensual. She closed her eyes and laid her head back. But instead of fantasizing about Bobby, she began to think of Lee.

Lee was a good-looking man. He was a little taller than she was. He had nice big hands. She'd noticed his hands when they were out in the vineyards. The way he held his camera. His weren't as rough and calloused as Bobby's hands. Lee's hands were smooth. Hands that did not do farm work.

And suddenly she was fantasizing about Bobby again. How his rough hands would caress her smooth skin. Laura's eyes flew open. She did not want to think about Bobby and how rude and irritating he was.

She settled back in the water, running more hot water in the tub, feeling the jets of water caress her skin. Laura closed her eyes and began to think of Lee again. She hoped his big hands equated to other big things on his body.

Once again, the washcloth soothed her skin. She ran the cloth again between her legs, paying attention to the sensitive spot between her legs. She swirled in the tub, opening her legs and moving in such a way that she could feel one of the jets reach her clitoris as well.

Laura worked herself into an orgasm and felt the release flood through her being.

As the water cooled, Laura got out of the tub and reached again for the white plush robe. Would a Holiday Inn have these? Probably not.

She dried off and decided she'd better figure out where she would live for the next couple of weeks.

Laura donned her light-yellow silk pajamas and pulled out her laptop to see what hotels were near the winery. She found a Hampton Inn and Suites nearby. That might be more in her budget. And she could use some of her Hilton points. Laura knew she wouldn't get the soft sheets of her B&B at any Hilton property.

Around 7 p.m., Laura decided she was hungry. She didn't really want to get dressed again, but even ordering out meant still having to pick up the order, unless she wanted pizza. And she did not want pizza. But she checked a local pizza place and found it had salads, some pasta dishes, and garlic bread that she could order as takeout.

Laura decided on a salad, baked ziti, and garlic bread. She still had that unopened bottle of Cabernet from Star 1. She dressed and picked up the food, bringing the meal back to the B&B.

She asked for a corkscrew and wine glass at the reception desk and carried both up the stairs to her room.

As Laura got back into her silk pajamas, removed her bra and got situated, she realized she should have asked for a plate and cutlery from the reception desk, too.

She ended up eating out of the takeout boxes with a plastic fork. She realized the order was more than she could eat.

In her pajamas, she peeked out into the hall with her leftovers, looking for a trash can. She didn't want the food smelling up her room.

Laura walked quickly down the stairs, spotted a trash can and dumped the food. She did not make eye contact with anyone in the lounge area reading books or playing checkers. She could feel their eyes on her, though.

She smiled at the thought. She knew she had a beautiful body and the pale silk barely hid her dark nipples. The men were probably looking at her admiringly and the women were frowning with jealousy.

Laura returned to her room and drank another glass of the wine. She corked it with about a glass and a half left, saving something for tomorrow's meal, although she'd try to remember to grab a better vintage from Star 1.

Laura dreaded leaving the B&B. But what could she do? Should she tell Quitman she was moving to a hotel? Would he even care? She'd let Bobby and Lee know. Then she sighed. She doubted they would care either.

Bobby Pierce finished the last of his work just as the sun was setting. He was filthy and tired. He walked into his house and headed straight for the shower, dropping his dirty clothes on the floor. He let the water run until it heated up before he stepped in.

After scrubbing his skin and washing his hair, Bobby wrapped a towel around his waist and walked out into his small living room. The quilt from his bed was draped across his armchair. He picked it up to return it to the bedroom and could smell Laura's perfume on it. His towel began to rise.

"Oh no," Bobby muttered to himself. "Don't even think about her. She's nothing but trouble."

He put on his gym shorts and a sweatshirt and poured himself a beer. Sitting down at his kitchenette table, Bobby began checking his emails and voicemails from the day. He answered several that night. He'd call back the people who left voicemails tomorrow morning.

Bobby was hungry and made a bologna and mayonnaise sandwich on white bread, eating it in just a few bites. He grabbed an apple from the countertop and bit in, polishing it off quickly. He swallowed the rest of his beer and walked out his side door to put the bottle in the recycle bin.

He sat in his leather recliner and turned on his television with the remote. He clicked through several channels before he found a San Francisco Giants baseball game. Bobby awoke two hours later, the ball game over, and with a pain in his neck.

Bobby got up slowly, stretched, shut off the television and lights and headed to bed. As he pulled the quilt over him, he fell asleep smelling Laura's perfume.

Laura got online the next morning and made a reservation for the Hampton Inn. At least she got a king bed and would still get breakfast every morning.

Then she texted Lee to see what time the models would be arriving Tuesday at the winery. He texted back three men and three women of different ages and ethnicities were scheduled to arrive shortly after lunch. He wanted to use the afternoon light.

Well, that's good, Laura thought. I won't have to feed them either.

Lee texted that the models were bringing rented tuxedos, wedding dresses, and casual clothes that they'd wear depending on the shoot. He'd told them to bring their receipts for Laura to invoice.

Laura got dressed and headed over to the winery to make sure they'd have somewhere to change clothes and to see about the rental tables and chairs for the shoots. When she learned the photo shoot would be Tuesday, she'd gotten the tables and chairs to arrive that day, too.

She'd leave it all set up for when the reporter arrived the next day. It was all coming together, she thought. Laura sighed her relief.

Laura parked her rental car near the front of the office and walked in to find Bobby at his desk.

"Oh good, I caught you here," she said.

"Why wouldn't I be here?"

"Well, you could have been out in the vines again. Listen, the models are coming this afternoon and I need a place where they can change into their costumes. Can we use this office?"

"And where am I going to go?" Bobby asked, annoyed.

"Go check your grapes. We'll probably be shooting all afternoon. We'll use the event space and probably go out into the vineyard, too."

"You're going to shoot out in the fields? How many people are there?"

"Six models, the photographer and me," she replied.

"I don't want that many people tramping around in the fields," he growled. "I don't want the vines broken."

"We won't break your precious vines."

"Damn straight you won't. I'm going with you to make sure you don't."

"I don't need you there," she said, then paused. "You don't trust me, do you?"

"You? Of course not."

"You're an ass."

"So you've told me."

Laura threw up her hands and exhaled loudly. "You are impossible!"

The furniture rental truck arrived. Laura met the drivers and showed them the event space. The drivers then began unloading the chairs and tables as Laura directed how she wanted them placed.

Laura had purchased some inexpensive white tablecloths and put them over the round wooden tables. She had some extras and covered some of the chairs. She wished she'd thought to get some wide ribbon to tie the tablecloths around the chairs.

She'd found a craft store and bought some plastic grapes, confetti and tea candles for the tables. She'd also found white fairy lights. She'd need a hammer and some nails to put the lights up.

As the delivery men returned to their truck, she told them they could come back Thursday morning to pick everything up. Then Laura went in search of Bobby to see if she could borrow some tools.

"Hey, I'm sure you have a hammer and nails," she said when she found him. "Can I borrow them?"

"What do you need those for?"

"I need to string some white fairy lights in the event space. And I have to run back to the store to get some ribbon to tie back the chair covers. Unless you have some of that."

"I don't have any ribbon. I've got twine to train some of the vines."

"Oh, that might be even better. Give the space a rustic look."

"Rustic look," Bobby muttered. He left Laura standing in the office and returned with a hammer and some nails. "Do you need a ladder?"

"I think I can just stand on a chair…" she started to say.

"Let me get you a proper ladder. I don't want you to fall and break an ankle."

"I'm delighted you are so concerned with my safety," Laura said with sarcasm.

"Lady, you could break your neck for all I care. You'd ride away in an ambulance and be out of my life for good. But I don't want you to sue the winery because of your carelessness."

Why was Bobby always making her life so difficult? Laura wondered.

"Just give me the damned ladder," she snapped.

Bobby brought a six-foot ladder and set it up in the event space. He then handed the hammer and several nails to Laura.

Laura, who was wearing a skirt, blouse and her boots, began to climb the ladder with the hammer and some nails in her hand. She got about halfway up and tried to reach up to hammer in a nail on some door trim. She started to lose her balance and felt Bobby's hands grab her at the hips.

"You're going to fall," he said. "Climb down. I'll do that. Can't trust you to do a man's job."

Laura narrowed her eyes at him. "I am quite capable of doing a man's job, as you call it. It's hammering in some nails. Not that hard."

"Get down," he commanded. "I'll do this."

Laura got off the ladder and put her hands on her hips.

"Now don't get all huffy," Bobby said, climbing up the ladder. "Give me the hammer."

Laura wanted to pound it into his head, but instead put it in his hand.

"Now the nails."

She handed those over.

"Tell me where you want to hang those lights," Bobby said.

"Start at that corner," Laura said, pointing to one corner of the room. "I've got several strings of lights, so we should have enough to go all the way around."

Bobby hammered a couple of nails, got off the ladder, moved it and began the process again. Laura pulled a chair over, stood on it and began hanging the first strand of lights.

"Hey, don't do that. I don't want you to fall," Bobby said, watching Laura climb on the chair across the room.

"I'll be fine," she said, as the chair wobbled under her. "OK. This isn't all that steady."

Bobby pulled the ladder around and climbed up, taking the string of lights and wrapping it around the nails. He continued around the room until all the lights were strung.

"OK, plug them in," he said.

Laura plugged in the lights and it caught her breath. "They are so pretty. You had some the night of the party. That's what I wanted to recreate."

"There were lights at the party?"

"Yes, don't you remember?"

"I wasn't really paying attention. The catering company I hired did all that. I was busy working the event."

"Shit, you should have told me that. I'd have hired them to do it all again."

"Well, you didn't ask me. I can't read your mind."

Laura smiled. Good thing you can't read my mind, she thought.

"What's the smile for?" he asked.

"I was just thinking it's a good thing you can't read my mind. You'd be dead and buried somewhere in your fields."

Bobby's face darkened. "Well, that's what I get for helping you," he said, pushing himself off the wall he'd been leaning against. "It won't happen again." He began walking back to his office.

"I'm sorry," Laura said, following him, grabbing him by the arm. "I really appreciate your help this morning. Thank you, Bobby."

Bobby turned and looked down into Laura's brown eyes. Bobby's face softened a bit. "You're welcome. Let me know when you and your parade go to the fields. I'm going with you."

"Suit yourself, but we really don't need an escort."

"Laura, don't go without me. This winery is my responsibility."

"OK. We won't leave without you."

The models arrived ahead of Lee Adams. Laura showed them the event space where they'd be shooting most of the photos. She also told them they would likely go out later in the day into the vineyard for some candid shots among the vines.

"Do we have a trailer to change in?" a younger model named Suzy asked.

"We don't have a trailer. I've secured the office where everyone can take turns changing in there," Laura said, showing them to the office. She opened the door and Bobby turned around to see the faces of the models crowding the door and looking at him.

"Well, hello, handsome," Suzy said.

"Ah, Bobby will not be here when you are changing," Laura said, shooting a dark look at Bobby.

"Too bad," Suzy replied, wiggling her eyebrows.

"Is there another room we can use?" a younger model named Brett asked. "The women can use this and us guys can use another one."

"Follow me," Bobby said, heading to his house. The men followed Bobby, who opened his door and told them they could change in there.

Lee, who had been setting up lights in the event space, came around to the office, knocked on the door and asked two women to dress in wedding attire. He then headed to the house and asked two men to don tuxedoes.

Lee wanted to mix and match the couples, so he'd shoot some same sex couples and some traditional couples. The other woman he asked to dress in a cocktail dress and the man he asked to dress in khakis and a sports coat. He'd use them as background characters.

"Hey, can you and Bobby be background characters too?" Lee asked. "Laura, your outfit is perfect. Bobby, do you have anything, ah, dressier?"

Bobby frowned. "Hey, I don't want to get all dressed up. I'm not in your show."

"Bobby, please," Laura pleaded. "We'd just be in the background. We might not even use any of the photos that you are in."

"If you won't use them, why do I have to be in them?"

"We really just need bodies," Lee explained. "Do any of your workers want to be extras, as it were?"

"You'd have to ask them. They're all here in work clothes though," Bobby said.

"OK. Well, if you have some khaki pants and a sports coat, you'll do," Lee said.

"I'm so glad 'I'll do,'" Bobby sneered.

Lee rolled his eyes. He was used to dealing with prima donnas, but Bobby wasn't a celebrity. He was just a jerk, Lee thought.

Bobby disappeared into his house and came out with dark khaki pants, a blue cotton shirt and a dark navy sports coat. Laura was shocked at how well he cleaned up. She thought he'd even run a comb through his brown hair.

Lee directed couples to stand under the fairy lights, shooting a variety of couples. Older and younger models together, same sex couples together, mixed race couples together. He had them holding wine glasses filled with some Star 1 wines, all looking lovingly at each other.

Laura, Bobby and the character models stood as background guests, shaking the hands of the grooms, or hugging the brides.

When Lee was satisfied that he'd shot enough of the same brides and grooms, he had the models change clothes and shot different couples.

"This is boring," Bobby said, standing next to Laura.

"Well, this is what modeling work is like."

"What do you know about modeling life? Were you a model?"

"Oh no, but I've been on publicity shoots like this. It's a lot of hurry up and wait."

"Well, I'm ready for a beer."

"You're at your winery. Better make it a glass of wine," Laura said. "Get another bottle and have everyone crowd around like we're celebrating the couple."

"Great idea, Laura," Lee said. "Can we do that, Bobby?"

"I'm invoicing you for this wine," Bobby told Laura, pointing at her.

"Fine. But it will show off the wine."

Lee shot scenes of the couples celebrating, then directed the models to put on more casual clothes to move down into the vineyard. He wanted to catch the afternoon light. "Bring your glasses and a couple bottles of the wine. Bobby, do you have a picnic blanket or any kind of blanket we can use as a prop?"

"You've got that quilt," Laura told Bobby.

"You are not using my grandmother's quilt," Bobby barked.

"OK. No grandmother's quilt," Lee said. "Any other blanket?"

"I'll look in the shed," Bobby said, coming back out with a filthy blanket.

"That probably won't do," Lee said. "Let me see what I have in my truck."

Lee went to his truck and rummaged in the camper. He pulled out a silver sheet used for lighting. "This will have to do. Maybe we can photoshop it to make it look like a blanket."

The crowd began moving down to the fields, though didn't walk as long or far as Laura had to find Bobby a few days ago. Lee stopped them just a few yards down and set the silver sheet down between a row of vines.

"Be careful. Do not break any of the vines," Bobby cautioned.

Lee directed one set of couples to sit on the silver sheet and pose with the wine glasses. He switched out several couples so he had a variety.

"Now you two," Lee said to Bobby and Laura.

"What? You've got plenty of other people, I don't need to…" Bobby began.

"Please, Bobby. Do this and we're done," Laura said.

Bobby looked at Lee. "We're done after this? You'll all go home?"

"Sure," the photographer replied.

Bobby and Laura sat on the sheet and took the wine glasses that had been passed around the among the various models. There was still a bit of wine in the glasses.

"Let's top those off," Lee said, handing Laura the wine bottle. Laura dumped her wine on the ground then poured a new glass.

"That's a waste of my wine," Bobby said, but he did the same.

Laura poured more wine into his glass.

"Now look at each other like you love each other," Lee directed.

Bobby laughed. "You've got to be kidding."

"Bobby, here is your chance at an Oscar. Just act like you like me," Laura said.

Bobby and Laura faced each other, smiling, laughing. Lee directed Bobby to caress Laura's hair, touch her neck.

"Would you mind giving each other a kiss?" Lee asked.

Bobby leaned in as if to kiss Laura and whispered, "I wish I'd eaten onions for lunch."

"You are a snake, Bobby Pierce," she whispered back, cupping his cheek, pretending that they were a loving couple.

"Alright, you two. I think I've got what I need."

"Thank God," Bobby said, pushing away from Laura and standing up. He gulped the glass of wine in his hand.

Brett walked over, took Laura's hand and helped her stand up. They picked up the silver blanket, gathered the glasses and empty wine bottles and all walked back to the event space.

"I'll have these prints to you in a flash drive by Thursday," Lee said to Laura as they walked back.

"Thanks. I've got a reporter coming tomorrow. I hope Bobby will behave. I haven't told him she wants to interview him, too."

Lee let out a low whistle. "You have your hands full with that one."

"I do. He's like a toddler."

"Well, I'll swing by on Thursday. Maybe we can do some photos out in the field of you."

"Don't you have all that you need?"

"Well, I don't have any of just you, Laura."

"Oh, OK. I thought you did have some from before."

"I'd like to get just a few more," he said.

Laura wasn't sure what Lee was after, but she started to have an uneasy feeling about him.

Chapter 8

When everyone had left, she'd worked at her desk in Bobby's office for another hour before she gathered her things to go back to the B&B.

She hadn't seen Bobby since she'd talked to Lee by his truck. She thought maybe he'd be in the office, but she was the only one there. She assumed he'd gone to his house.

Laura thought about knocking on the door to say goodbye but thought better of it. He clearly didn't like her and let her know at every turn.

She climbed into her rental car, stopped at a Thai restaurant and ordered takeout, and headed to her room. She was glad she'd found a half bottle of wine on a table in the event space. She'd liberated it and planned to have it with her spicy Thai food.

Laura set up her takeout boxes on the small desk in her room, pulled out her plastic fork and spoon. She was glad she'd found this restaurant. It reminded her of one of her favorite Thai restaurants in Atlanta, Nan in Midtown.

She ordered panang curry with chicken, asking that it be pretty spicy. The chicken was a little dry. Laura sighed. She should have eaten at the restaurant, but she just wanted to put on her silk pajamas. The fried pork egg rolls were good and the curry was pretty spicy. Maybe too spicy. The red wine tasted good with her meal.

Laura eyed the tub again. She'd better take advantage of it until she had to leave in three days. But first, she crept down the stairs of the B&B and tossed the remainder of her meal.

She got back in her room and opened her laptop again, answering a few emails and emailing the reporter to be sure she was coming the next day. She included directions to the winery.

Laura logged off and realized she was too tired for a bath. She just wanted to sleep. She shut everything down, undressed and slipped under the soft cotton sheets. They felt cool against her skin, but the duvet would help warm her up. She drifted off to sleep thinking of how Bobby's hands had felt around her hips.

Laura awoke with a start, sweaty and scared. Her heart raced. It was the same nightmare she'd had ever since her attack decades ago. Julio smiling at her while he struck her over and over.

She got out of bed on shaky legs and reached for her handbag for the anti-anxiety pills she always carried. She popped the pill in her mouth and got a glass from the bathroom. Filling it with water, she swallowed the bitter pill.

Laura knew it would be a while before she'd be able to go back to sleep. She turned on the TV in her room and turned the volume down low. She clicked through the channels unable to concentrate on any dull late-night show or reruns, so she turned off the TV.

Then she opened her laptop and got back in bed. She decided she should learn as much as she could about Bobby Pierce.

There wasn't much to find. He didn't have a Facebook page or a Twitter account. He really should have an Instagram account, she thought. He should be posting as many photos as he could. She'd suggest that to him and a Facebook page for Start 1.

She rolled her eyes. He'd probably think that was beneath him and tell her publicity was her job. She could do it for him, but she'd have to wrangle Kyle Quitman to let that be part of her regular job. She wasn't going to do it for free.

She also looked up his formal name, Robert Pierce. Now this is interesting, she said to herself as she found a Robert Pierce on a people finder site. She wasn't going to pay to find out more, but it had his age, 51, and a list of his relatives, including his ex-wife. He was older than she expected. He certainly didn't look like he was in his 50s.

There could be other Robert Pierces in California. She was sure there were, because it wasn't an uncommon name, but the one she found listed his address at the winery. She quickly wrote it down, since maybe that would be an address to give the reporter if she got lost.

Then, because she was curious, Laura looked up Lee Adams. That one was harder because there were lots of people named Lee Adams in California on the internet. But she did find his Facebook page, his Instagram account and a Twitter feed.

Yes, Lee, she thought, you know more about social media and business than Bobby does.

Lee had a lot of photos on his IG account. Some were professional and business related, but she enjoyed seeing the photos of dogs, flowers, interesting architecture, too. He really had a good eye. No wonder he was a photographer.

She also found a more personal photo. One of Lee and a woman. It looked like a girlfriend, or maybe his wife. He had his arm draped around her waist. A very intimate pose.

Hmm. It kind of made Laura more interested in him. Forbidden goods. Maybe there would be more fantasizing about Lee in the bathtub tomorrow. He was very good looking. And younger than Bobby, she thought.

Maybe she should turn her full attention to Lee. He'd probably be a nice distraction.

No more fantasizing about Bobby, she thought. He's not interested in her and he's an asshole. She needed to finish this job and head back to Atlanta. She just hoped she made money with this gig and could return home soon.

Laura looked at the small digital clock on the nightstand by her bed. It read 3:34 a.m. She laid back down and hoped she'd get back to sleep and the nightmare wouldn't return.

It had felt so real. That was the scariest part. She could feel the sting of Julio's hand on her cheek as he slapped her.

Laura's phone alarm went off and she dragged herself out of her bed. She'd need several coffees to get her started this morning.

She showered, dressed and headed down for the breakfast at the B&B, stopping first at the coffee station. She asked if they could make an espresso. When told they didn't have any, Laura asked for coffee as strong as they could make it.

She made a point to be sure to find a Starbucks and get an espresso on the way to the winery. She had eggs benedict, toast and some fresh-squeezed orange juice. She was told the eggs came from free range hens on a farm near the B&B.

Laura knew she wasn't going to get free-range eggs at Hampton Inn, so she enjoyed every bite.

When she finished breakfast, she went back to her room, gathered her laptop and got into her rental car, stopping by a Starbucks drive-thru for something stronger than the coffee at the B&B.

She pulled up to the winery and parked near the office. Laura had no idea what kind of mood Bobby was going to be in that morning, but she wasn't going to put up with any of his bullshit. She was tired, and in a foul mood herself.

Laura entered the office to find Bobby already at his desk, coffee mug in hand.

"Good morning, sunshine," he said, turning to her with a cheesy grin on his face.

"Bite me," she replied.

"Well, you're in a good mood today."

"I did not sleep well last night. And that reporter is coming today. I've got to be on top of my game and you do too."

"Me? Why me?"

"She wants to interview you."

"That wasn't part of the deal. Besides, I'm busy today. One of the models called this morning. She thinks she left her sunglasses behind. She's coming up to get them."

"Sunglasses? That's the oldest ploy in the book to meet up again," Laura said.

"Maybe, but here they are," he answered, holding a pair of Oakley sunglasses.

"Well tell her you're busy today and to come tomorrow."

"Can't. She's got another modeling gig so she's coming today."

"Bobby, I need you to be here for the reporter. Can't you leave them somewhere for her to get? Like the mailbox at the end of the driveway?"

"What time is the reporter getting here?"

"About one o'clock."

"Perfect. Suzy will be here at 2:30. I'll have plenty of time for your thing and then meet with Suzy."

Suzy? Laura had hoped the model coming to retrieve her sunglasses was the older woman. Suzy was young, pretty and a bottle blonde. She'd seen the way Suzy had looked at Bobby during the photo shoot. Laura realized Suzy probably had left the sunglasses behind on purpose.

"Well, I'd like to go over some talking points with you about the winery, what you should highlight, like the event space. And you'll need to put on some nice clothes."

Bobby looked down at himself. He had on faded blue jeans and his favorite navy plaid flannel shirt. "What's wrong with this?" he asked.

"Wear those khaki pants you had on yesterday and a polo shirt. That light blue one was nice."

"You're dressing me now? Are you my mother? Besides, those pants got dirty yesterday. We were sitting on the ground, remember?"

"I remember. You only have one pair of nice pants?" Laura asked in disbelief. Every man she knew in Atlanta had a closet full of khaki pants, in different colors no less.

"I like to wear jeans, ok?"

"Well, hurry up and put those pants in the washer so they'll be ready when Kimberly Gifford comes."

"Who's Kimberly Gifford?"

"The reporter. I just told you that."

"You never told me her name," Bobby said, breaking into a wide smile. "Two women want my attention today. This is my lucky day."

Laura rolled her eyes at him. "Oh my God, get over yourself."

"Just saying, I'm a hot commodity," he said, winking and walking back to his house.

Kimberly Gifford arrived shortly before 1 p.m., parking her Jeep Wrangler next to Laura's rental car. It made Laura's small Chevy look like a toy car by comparison.

Laura met her outside and walked her toward the office, where Bobby was seated in his newly washed khaki pants and a light green polo shirt.

Bobby shook Kimberly's hand and turned on the charm. Laura could see Kimberly beam at the handsome winery owner.

Well, if Bobby's charm could get them a nice article in the local community paper, so be it, Laura thought.

Bobby gave Kimberly a short tour of the winery, mentioning the points Laura had wanted him to go over. Laura trailed behind them on the tour like a puppy. She was once again glad she had worn her boots.

When they were done, he brought her to the event space, still set up with tables, chairs and the white fairy lights. Bobby turned on the lights and Kimberly's eyes got wide.

"Oh, that's beautiful," she said. "I could see myself here with a group of girlfriends."

"Yes," Laura interjected. "A girlfriends brunch would be a wonderful use of this space. Same for bridal showers, baby showers, wedding receptions, or even family reunions."

Kimberly was scribbling furiously in her notebook but kept looking up at Bobby.

As the hour approached two o'clock, Bobby tried to end the interview. "I'm sorry Kimberly, I have another appointment in just a few minutes."

Laura watched Kimberly's face fall, then perk up, asking, "Well, can I have your cell number? Just in case I have any follow up questions."

"Kimberly, can you run those questions by me?" Laura asked.

But Bobby interrupted, giving Kimberly his cell number. He caught a flash of anger in Laura's eyes. He smiled at Kimberly and then at Laura. "Call any time if you have any questions. When can I expect to see your wonderful article about Star 1?"

"I'm going to talk to my editor, but I think it will be a nice Sunday feature in the middle of June," she said. Kimberly turned to Laura. "You said you've got some high-resolution photos we can use?"

"Yes. We had publicity photos shot last week and yesterday. I have your email so I can send you a Dropbox link," Laura answered. "But I'd appreciate it if you'd run any follow-up questions by me, please."

Kimberly shook her head in assent, but Laura knew she'd likely never hear from her again. She was going to call Bobby. Laura was sure of it.

Kimberly's Jeep was kicking up dust down the driveway when Suzy's silver Lexus passed her.

Suzy Skelton also pulled up next to Laura's rental, making Laura wish she had parked her car behind one of the outbuildings.

"Hey, Laura, isn't it?" Suzy said, bouncing out of her car.

Laura was too tired now for her fake enthusiasm. Laura nodded at her.

"Is Bobby here? He told me he found my sunglasses."

"The ones you left behind? On purpose?" Laura said bluntly.

Suzy looked taken aback, unsure if she heard Laura correctly. "Oh no. Not on purpose. I love those sunglasses. I'm glad Bobby found them."

"Well, let me take you to him," Laura said with a fake smile, turning on her bootheel and striding briskly into the office.

"Look who's here," Laura said. "Your friend who left her sunglasses behind."

Bobby stood up and grabbed the Oakley sunglasses and started to hand them to Suzy, who had held her hand out to shake hands. Bobby quickly put the glasses in his left hand and reached out for Suzy. Laura noticed they shook hands just a little longer than necessary.

"Oh, thank you. I'm so glad you found them. They are really my favorite pair. I lost the last ones I had," Suzy gushed.

"I know you've seen the winery, but why don't I give you a private tour?" Bobby said, giving Suzy a big smile. "The afternoon sun is particularly lovely in the fields."

He began to steer Suzy on the path that led down to the fields. Laura started to trail along before Bobby turned to her. "Don't you have more public relations work to do? Kyle will want a report."

Laura stopped, gaped at Bobby who had turned his attention back to Suzy, then turned and strode back to the office. She cursed him as she walked. She hoped he heard her.

Chapter 9

About two hours later, Bobby and Suzy finally walked back up the path and toward the office. Laura had been watching at the door, and quickly sat at her desk, trying to look disinterested.

As they walked through the door, Laura heard Bobby tell Suzy, "Well, I'm looking forward to dinner tonight. I'll pick you up at seven. Is that OK?"

"That is fine. Thanks again, Bobby. I loved the tour. You are so passionate about what you do. I'll text you my address and see you tonight."

Suzy smiled a fake smile at Laura and returned to her car.

Suzy was barely out the door when Laura exploded. "You're going out with her?"

"Yes. She's very interesting. And it's just dinner. Don't tell me you are jealous."

"I am not jealous of you. You do whatever you want. Besides, I'm seeing Lee tonight," Laura lied.

"You're seeing that photographer? I thought he was gay."

"He's not gay. He has — or rather had — a girlfriend," Laura said.

"And now he has you."

"Now he has me for a dinner date. Enjoy your evening, Bobby."

Laura got in her rental car and immediately called Lee. She hadn't planned to ask him out, but with Bobby seeing Suzy that night she didn't want to be alone. She hated to admit she was jealous.

Laura got Lee's voicemail. "Hey, Lee, it's Laura. I wondered if you were free tonight for dinner. I'm tired of eating alone at various restaurants. I'd love some company and we can go over those photos. I'll expense the meal, so my treat."

She hoped that would be convincing enough to make Lee agree to dinner tonight. She got back to the B&B, took a nice hot shower to get the dust of the winery off her skin and made a cup of coffee in her room.

By the time she reached for her phone, she saw she had a voicemail message. It was Lee's number. She returned the call without listening to the message. If he was declining her offer of dinner tonight, she'd try to convince him otherwise.

"Lee, I see you called," Laura said. "I didn't listen to the message, so I hope you have a restaurant in mind for dinner tonight."

"Laura, I have plans for early evening, but could do a late dinner. Is that OK?"

"Oh, that will be fine," Laura said, shaking her head. She realized she'd have to try to take a short nap. She'd never make a late dinner without it. She looked down at her cup of coffee and realized that was a mistake if she were going to try to nap. She walked into the bathroom and poured it down the sink. "What time are you thinking?"

"How about 9:30? I could pick you up."

"That would be perfect. I'll see you at 9:30."

Laura quickly undressed, put on her sleep mask and tried to take a short nap. She'd set her alarm for 8:30 to give herself a full hour to get ready. But she tossed and turned. She could not and did not fall asleep.

Finally, she flung the covers off and sat up in bed. Maybe she should read. That sometimes made her tired.

She got up and got out her e-reader and scanned several finance and business books she'd been meaning to read. Then she turned to a spy thriller by Daniel Silva, "The English Spy." She'd been meaning to read it since it came out a year ago.

She started reading and before she knew it her alarm was going off. It was time to get ready for her late-night date.

Laura redressed and reapplied her makeup. She did her hair and waited for Lee to call to say he'd arrived. Nine thirty came and went and she now doubted he was going to keep her date. When he did call a little after ten, Laura was sure he was calling to cancel.

"Laura, I'm sorry to be so late. I didn't expect traffic this time of night, but it is California. I should be there in about 20 minutes. Do you still want to go out?"

"I'd love to. I'm famished. Will the restaurants still be open?" Laura asked. She knew in Atlanta many restaurants closed by 11 p.m. on weeknights.

"Oh, I know a diner that's really good. It stays open pretty late. I thought we'd go there."

"Sounds good. I'll see you soon," Laura replied. Diner? What the hell?

Laura sighed. She wished she hadn't called Lee and just had gone out to dinner alone tonight. She thought she was way overdressed for a diner and would probably only be able to get a sandwich. Some nice dinner, she scowled.

Lee arrived around 10:30 p.m. Laura was exhausted but climbed into his truck and Lee drove to the Midnight Diner. Laura was surprised it was busy.

"It's a good place to come after a movie or the theater," Lee said as they were seated.

"What's good here?"

"They make a great Reuben," Lee said.

aura laughed. "No one makes a great Reuben outside of New York City."

"Suit yourself, but that's what I always get."

Laura looked over the menu. It was pretty typical diner fare. Open-faced sandwiches, salads, hamburgers. She decided on a Cobb salad since anything heavy would keep her awake later that night, or rather early that morning. She couldn't imagine they'd leave before midnight.

They talked about the photo shoot they'd just completed. Lee brought a contact sheet with a series of the photos and marked the ones he thought would be good for the newspaper article Kimberly Gifford was doing. He also asked Laura if they could take a drone up to make a nice video of the property.

"How much more will that cost? Because that would be awesome for the Star 1 website," she said.

"It won't be too much more. I'll send you an email with the cost. It will take me a while to edit the video, but it would be great to get the entire property."

Laura smiled at Lee. He was a true salesman, adding more to the work he could do and what he could charge.

Laura and Lee left the diner shortly before 1 a.m.

"I'm not usually out this late on a weeknight when I've got work to do tomorrow," she said as they got back into Lee's truck. Laura stifled a yawn.

But they'd had dinner, then dessert and decaf coffee. Laura couldn't resist the key lime pie. She was hoping it would be as delicious as the ones she'd had in Miami.

Her dessert wasn't the way she remembered her mother had made the pie, tart and sweet and with real key limes. Still, she'd have a very pleasant evening with Lee, and she hadn't had to eat alone.

When Lee stopped at Laura's B&B, she thanked him for joining him for dinner and he thanked her for paying for it.

Laura got out and went up to her room. It had been a very long day.

Laura hadn't set her alarm for the next morning. She wanted one day to sleep in the soft sheets before she cleared out the next day. She had booked the Hampton Inn for a week, then would reassess whether she needed another week. She was praying her trip wouldn't have to be extended. She was tired of doing battle with Bobby. She was tired of shelling out money for the props, hear meals, everything. She was ready to go home.

Laura spent a lazy morning in her room, drinking coffee, taking a leisurely bath. This was likely the last jetted bathtub she'd be in for a long while.

She finally got out, dried off and found a comfortable outfit for the winery. She'd long given up her skirts, dresses and high heels she'd brought for the trip.

Laura drove up to the winery and was surprised to see Bobby's vehicle not parked in front of the office. She knocked on the office door but got no answer.

A winery worker walked by. "You need in the office?"

Laura turned. She'd seen him before. Walker was it?

"Yes. I don't see Bobby's truck. Is he here?"

"He hasn't shown up yet. You'll have to wait."

Laura got back into her rental car and began making calls to some other publications and checked in with Kimberly Gifford about when the Star 1 winery feature would run in her paper.

Around noon, Laura heard a truck rumble up outside the office. She looked up. She saw Bobby unlock the office door and stride in. She got out of her car and followed him in.

"You're here late," she said, brightly.

"Oh, I had a great night with Suzy and it's a great morning!"

Laura frowned. A great night with Suzy? What did that mean? Did he sleep with her?

"And how was your date with Lee?" Bobby asked, flopping down in his office chair.

Laura noticed he was wearing the clothes he'd worn yesterday. Although to be honest he always wore jeans and some sort of plaid flannel shirt. But he was unshaven. That wasn't a good sign.

"I had a great night, although we got home very early this morning," Laura said, trying to gauge Bobby's reaction.

"Well, good for you. I hope your nighttime activities have left you well rested. I feel like a new man," Bobby said, stretching his arms over his head.

"I have no idea what you're talking about," Laura said. "I had a wonderful night with Lee, but there were no 'nighttime activities' as you called them. We had a wonderful evening together."

"Well, I had some lovely nighttime activities with Suzy and I feel great," Bobby said, rubbing his face. "I should probably go shave."

Laura's frown got deeper. Bobby slept with Suzy? She was not happy about that. Bobby looked like a prized rooster the way he had strutted into the office. She was pissed that he'd taken her to task for giving the caterer a blow job and yet he was proud that he'd slept with Suzy.

Typical double standard, Laura thought. She'd like to wipe that smug smile off his face.

"You look like you've swallowed a lemon. Why the sourpuss face?" Bobby asked.

"As if you didn't know."

"I don't know. What's wrong with you?"

"You are such a hypocrite," Laura exploded, getting up from her chair, her hands balled into fists.

"Hypocrite? What are you talking about?"

"You give me shit for giving that guy a blow job and you come in here today crowing about having slept with Suzy. You are such a hypocrite. It's fine for you but not for me?"

Bobby's smile got bigger. "I didn't know you cared."

"I don't care," Laura shouted. "It just pisses me off you have a double standard when it comes to women."

"I don't have a double standard, Laura," Bobby said, raising his voice now too.

"Really? Well, why don't you mansplain it to me."

"Mansplain? What the fuck does that mean?"

"It means you are going to tell me why you can have sex with someone and I can't."

"I never said you couldn't have sex with anyone! Go out and fuck anyone you want! What I said was you couldn't have sex with any of my workers."

"And your caterers are your workers? I don't recall seeing anyone younger than 20 on this property."

"Oh God, was that caterer even of legal age?"

"Well, I couldn't exactly ask his age with his dick in my mouth!"

Bobby threw up his hands in exasperation. "You are really a piece of work, you know that? You are completely unprofessional. I want you off my property now!"

"But I'm not finished!"

"Yes, you are!"

Laura stood up and grabbed her handbag and left the office for her rental car. Her mind was spinning. What was happening? Bobby couldn't fire her, only Kyle Quitman could. But she didn't know how much influence Bobby had with Kyle.

If only she'd kept her mouth shut. It was not the first time her temper had gotten her into trouble.

She'd better call Kyle and make sure she could still do her job out here, especially if she'd just made a hotel reservation for the next week.

And Lee wanted to take the drone up to shoot video of the winery. She knew she'd made a mistake picking a fight with Bobby.

She hated it, but she'd have to call him to apologize. If anything, he should be apologizing to me, she thought angrily. But she knew he'd never see it that way. He was stubborn and proud, just like she was.

Laura got back to her room at the B&B and pulled out her suitcase. She might as well start packing. When she'd calmed down, she called Bobby. It went to voicemail.

Laura rolled her eyes. Really, Bobby, not going to accept my call? She took a deep breath as she heard his rich baritone voice telling her to leave a message.

"Hey, Bobby. I'm sorry I got so angry. I really do need to come back to the winery tomorrow. Lee wants to shoot some drone video of the winery. Again, I'm sorry. Please let me know if it's OK for me to come back."

Laura clicked off her phone, angry that she'd had to sound so conciliatory.

She sat at the small desk in her room and finished out emails and proposals. She also emailed Kyle to give an update, telling him about the photo shoot with the models, the newspaper article she felt sure she'd secured and some of the proposals to other magazines. She told him she'd have to move to the Hampton Inn since the B&B was not able to accommodate another week for her. She assured him she was still working hard for him.

Laura went out for a quick sandwich but came back to the B&B to keep working. Her back and neck began to ache and she stretched in her chair.

Laura looked at her phone and saw it was getting late. Another night of ordering takeout. She was unhappy she wasn't able to enjoy the nice restaurants she'd read about in Napa. But she had some work still to do and called in an order for Chinese. When this trip was over, she was treating herself to lots of Atlanta restaurants.

Laura's phone pinged with a message from Bobby.

Sorry I snapped at you. It was wrong of me. You can come on the property anytime you need to.

Laura raised her eyes in surprise. He'd apologized! She couldn't believe it. Then she reread the message. He sort of apologized, she realized.

Laura thought about how she would respond. She needed Bobby's cooperation for her to get paid by Kyle and she didn't want to antagonize him either.

I'll be by tomorrow before noon if that's OK.

Suit yourself.

Well, Bobby was still his charming self, Laura thought. But at least she'd be able to meet Lee. She texted Lee that they could fly the drone the next day, any time after noon.

Lee responded that he'd be there.

Laura went to sleep feeling more confident about the next day.

Laura had another restless night of sleep. She was missing her bed in her condo with her condo's security system. She awoke several times by odd noises and feared someone was in her room. She finally got up and placed a chair under the doorknob to prevent anyone from entering her room.

Laura knew she was being ridiculous, but it made her feel better and she finally got some deep sleep. She awoke the next day not quite rested, but ready for the day.

Laura pulled up outside of the office and saw Bobby headed in. She beeped her horn at him. He looked up at her.

"Is everything OK between us?" she asked.

"You tell me," he replied.

Well, this wasn't a good start, Laura thought.

"Lee is coming later today with the drone to get some aerial footage of the winery. I thought it would be great to add it to the Star 1 winery website. Which reminds me, we need to update it to include the new offerings we'll have."

"What new offerings?" Bobby asked.

"The event space, the bridal showers, wedding showers, weddings. We need to get that up on the website and include links to caterers that can handle that sort of thing."

"You take care of that," he said. "I need to go back to the fields today. More repairs to the trellises need to be made."

"Fine, I'll take care of it. Do you have the password for the website? I'll need that to make changes."

Bobby stared at Laura blankly. "I don't have them."

"Well, who does?"

"I have no idea. Some young kid did the website for us several years ago. I guess maybe he has it."

Laura kept from rolling her eyes at Bobby. "Do you have his name? Phone number? I'll need to call to get that information."

Bobby sighed deeply. "It's in this office somewhere," he said, leading Laura into the office. "Guess I won't be going to the fields. I'm at your beck and call today, Your Highness." He made a mock bow at Laura.

"Bobby, just tell me where to look. I'll search for it and you go to the fields."

"That's just it. I don't know where to tell you to look. It's probably in that filing cabinet," he said, pointing to an old beige four-tiered, slightly rusted office filing cabinet that looked like it might have come from military surplus.

"Well, how would it be labeled? Office documents? Website stuff?"

"I have no idea."

Laura sighed. "You really need a little organization for this winery. I'll start going through these cabinets. You go to the fields. If I can't find anything useful, I'll text you and we can go through any files I can't figure out."

"Good luck."

Laura was glad she'd worn jeans that day since she was on her knees going through dusty files. Some didn't look like they'd been opened for ages and quite a few made her sneeze.

She finally found a folder labeled WordPress. She felt sure she'd found the website information. Instead, she found faded hand-written notes that were barely legible. She found a phone number and called it.

A woman's voice answered.

"Hello, I'm looking for a guy who put together the Star 1 Winery website. This number was listed on some of the paperwork. Is he there?"

"Lady, I don't know what you are talking about. This is a private cell number."

"Sorry," Laura said, but the woman had hung up.

Well shit, Laura thought. Now what? Since she knew it was a WordPress site, she tried calling customer service to see if they could help her. She was placed on hold almost immediately.

She also got on the WordPress website and opened a chat with a customer service representative in case that was quicker. It was.

Please help. I'm in a bind. I am the public relations representative for Star 1 Winery and we've lost the admin information and password for our website. Can you help me?

The customer service representative — Jeremy — asked Laura questions she couldn't answer. She knew she'd have to text Bobby the questions.

Hold on, she typed in the chat box. **I'm going to text the owner of the winery. Maybe he can answer these questions.**

Bobby, Laura texted. **I'm on with WordPress customer service. He's asking questions about the website I can't answer. Can you help?**

Laura didn't get a reply right away. He must be busy out in the fields, she sighed.

Hey, the owner is busy in the vineyard right now. I'll have to chat back later.

Well, I'm happy to help if I can. Just come back to chat back when you can so we can help with the admin privileges.

Laura logged off with "Jeremy," if that was his real name, and sat back in her chair. This had been a frustrating day and she looked up to see Lee tapping at the office door.

She'd been so involved with finding the files for the website she forgot he was coming that afternoon.

Laura waved him in. "Sorry, I lost track of time. I was trying to find the password to the website. It's likely lost and I've been trying to get WordPress customer service to help."

"Good luck with that. You might have to start over."

"Ugh. I don't want that. I'm not a website developer and we have the domain name. We can't give that up."

"I know a guy who is a website guru. He can probably help."

"Lee, I love that you are trying to be helpful but every time you make suggestions to make my life easier, it costs me money."

Lee laughed. "Well, aren't you billing that investor guy?"

"I will for this! Let me have the number of your guru."

Lee typed into his phone and sent the contact number, which popped up on Laura's phone.

"He's kind of young, but he's good," Lee said.

"OK. I'll call him tonight. Are you ready to fly the drone?"

"It's in the back of my truck."

Lee got the drone out of its case. He did some preliminary checks and with a whir, the drone flew above Lee and Laura's heads. Lee began to walk with the controls to the edge of the winery.

"I may have to walk into the winery. The range on the controls won't let me go all the way out to the far edge of the winery."

"Bobby said it was OK. I'll follow you."

Lee and Laura walked down the path that led into the winery fields. Lee kept his head down, watching the controls of the drone, while Laura looked up at the white robotic body overhead.

Bobby could hear a whir and looked up to see the drone moving above him. He saw Lee and Laura walking down the path and began to move out toward them.

"Hola!" Lee called out.

"Hey there. You've got the drone up," Bobby said.

"Yep. Stand back. I'll go ahead and land it."

"Please don't take out any vines," Bobby said, worried.

"No worries. I'm a pretty good drone operator."

The drone landed a few feet from where the trio stood. Lee went over and picked it up. "I probably have enough footage for a nice video. Is there anything else you want me to shoot with the drone, while I'm here?"

Bobby and Laura both said no.

Lee held the drone as if it were a fragile bird as they began to walk back to the office.

"Lee said he knew a guy that could help with the website, so hopefully that will be squared away soon," Laura told Bobby.

"Hope so. I don't remember anything about it."

"Oh, my guy should be able to help. Just call him tomorrow, Laura."

"Lee, you are turning out to be indispensable," Bobby said with sarcasm.

"Well, I just want to help Laura," Lee said. "And the winery, too," he said quickly.

"I'm sure you do," Bobby said flatly.

Chapter 10

After Lee had packed up his drone late that afternoon and driven off, Laura rounded on Bobby.

"You didn't have to be so rude to Lee," she said.

"What are you talking about?"

"All that shit about him wanting to help me. Listen, he's saving our hides with this website stuff. You can't remember anything and I'm locked out of being able to fix the website."

Bobby threw his hands up defensively. "I was not rude to him. You are so touchy these days. Is it that time of the month?"

Laura could not suppress her outrage. She clenched her fists.

"Listen, you piece of shit. That's none of your business. You give me hell about being unprofessional. Are you being professional with that question? No."

"OK, I'm sorry. That was uncalled for."

"You bet it was. In corporate America you'd be hauled before HR for a question like that. You really need some sexual harassment training."

"I said I was sorry. Just forget it."

Laura narrowed her eyes at Bobby. "As if I could. You have no idea how to treat a professional woman. It must just eat you alive that you have to work with a woman as your equal."

"You think you are my equal?" Bobby shouted. "You have no idea what it's been like trying to run this winery. There haven't been as many good years as there should have been. I worry about losing this winery all the time. And now Kyle Quitman comes in to save the day!" Bobby waved his arms. "He's a piece of shit, too. Comes in with all that money and then Marc and you show up to spy on me!"

"Spy on you? You're delusional. You need to see a doctor."

"You have no idea what it takes to run a business. I bet you have a sugar daddy to keep you funded."

"You think my life has been easy? Running my own business? It's kill what you eat in my world. Every day I scramble to find new clients and make my mortgage and pay my bills. A sugar daddy? Ha! Nobody pays my way, buster."

The pair were squaring off in the small office. The heat between them began to rise.

"There are days I'd like to break your neck," Laura said.

"Just try it, lady," Bobby shot back.

Laura grabbed him by the arm, pulling it behind his back, a move she'd learned in her self-defense class.

But Bobby was nearly a foot taller than Laura and parried with a move that spun Laura around and had her arm pinned behind her back.

Laura panicked, remembering when Julio had gripped her arms as he hit her. Suddenly she felt like a wild and feral animal fighting to get away, attacking and scratching at Bobby, trying to bite his arm.

"Hey, hey, Laura!" Bobby shouted at her. "Stop!" Bobby reached out and grabbed both of Laura's arms, holding them down at her sides so she couldn't scratch him. He could feel blood running down his left cheek.

Laura froze, her eyes wide with fear. Her heart was racing and she felt a flood of adrenaline. "Oh God!"

Bobby pulled Laura to him and kissed her hard. Laura kissed him right back, her tongue urgently finding his.

"Oh fuck," Bobby whispered.

"Yes, let's," she replied into his ear.

"Laura, this probably isn't…"

"A good idea? No, I'm sure it isn't."

But Bobby was opening the office door and moving them both to his house, kissing Laura the entire time. He was afraid she might think better of what she was doing and escape. He didn't want her to escape. He wanted her. And he was pretty sure she wanted him, too.

The pair got into his house and Bobby began to pull off Laura's shirt. There were way too many buttons. He wanted to rip the shirt off her. He started to pull off buttons and Laura protested. "Hey! I like this shirt."

"I'll buy you another one," he growled and the buttons ripped off.

"Damn sure you will. You are way over dressed. Take your pants off."

"Yes, ma'am," Bobby said, tripping as he tried to take his pants off over his boots. "Shit."

He pulled off his boots and then got his pants off. He was not wearing any underwear and Laura's eyes widened.

"Oh, you go commando! Come here."

Laura pulled him toward her as Bobby moved her toward his bed.

They fell into the bed on top of the quilt that covered it.

"Isn't this your heirloom quilt?" Laura asked with sarcasm. "We can't make love on that."

"The hell we can't."

"Bobby Pierce, what would your grandmother say?" Laura said, beginning to laugh.

Bobby stood up, pulled Laura to her feet, and ripped the quilt off the bed, letting it fall to the floor. "Satisfied?"

"When your dick is in me, I will be."

A growl came from the back of Bobby's throat. He pulled at Laura's jeans, her thong panties and unsnapped her lace bra. He looked at her perfect perky breasts, taking them in his rough and calloused hands. Laura shuddered at his touch, letting out a long breath that came out as an ooohhh.

"Oh," was all he could say, too. "You are so gorgeous."

Bobby began kissing her breasts, sucking her nipples. Then he began kissing down her stomach and finding her outer labia. He pulled them apart with his hands and began licking her clit.

Laura groaned with pleasure. This is what that idiot Greg wouldn't do. She was so glad Bobby knew how the hell to please a woman — how to please her.

Laura suddenly smiled thinking she was going to enjoy going down on Bobby. He was going to get an even better blow job than that blabbermouth caterer.

Laura reached for him, pulling Bobby up to kiss him. She could taste herself on his tongue. Laura smiled a little wicked smile at him, rolling him on his back and lowering herself toward his erect penis.

"I bet you've been waiting for this," she purred.

She took his penis in her mouth, opening to take him all the way. She began to suck and stroke his penis at the same time. Bobby groaned and put his hand on her head. But she didn't want him to cum in her mouth. She wanted him to cum inside her, so she moved to his balls, licking and sucking them.

Bobby's hand moved onto her head again. "Oh baby, slow down. I'm so near."

"OK," she said. Laura straddled him, easing him into her. She began to stroke her clit while she moved on top of him. "I'll go slow."

Laura began to grind slowly on Bobby, making sure there were long, slow strokes on top of him.

Even so, Bobby's breathing got heavier. Bobby pushed Laura off him and quickly flipped her over on her back. Laura gasped as he thrust back into her.

"Oh baby," he said as he moved her legs onto his shoulders, pressing deeper into her. Laura grabbed his arms. They were like tree stumps. She felt every straining muscle as he moved in her. She ran her hands over his colorful tattoos.

Laura could feel Bobby move deeper inside her. She let go of his left arm and began to roll her left thumb over her clit, feeling her orgasm begin to grow. Her breathing became heavy and erratic.

"Bobby, Bobby," she panted.

"I want to cum with you," he said so softly, Laura barely heard him.

Laura began to cry out her pleasure, squeezing his penis with every orgasm.

"Oh God!" Bobby barked.

Laura could feel his cum inside her, dripping out with every strong, deep stroke.

Bobby collapsed next to Laura, pulling her close and breathing hard.

Laura was trying to catch her breath as well. She'd had such a strong orgasm. She hadn't had one like that in a long while. She felt tears come to her eyes. She blinked them back. She certainly didn't want Bobby to think she was crying.

Laura cuddled in closer to Bobby. She wondered if he was a pillow talker or if he would roll over and go to sleep right away. Most men she slept with rolled over and slept right away. They weren't talkers after a good session of sex.

Laura heard the soft snuffle of Bobby's snores. Yes, he was asleep. She rolled over onto her right side and fell into a deep sleep, too.

Laura woke up with Bobby's arm around her and felt him begin to stir next to her. He rolled on his back, his arm coming off her.

"Evening," he said.

"It's a very good evening," she answered, rolling over to face him. "I hope you slept well."

"Like a log. You?"

"I always sleep well after great sex."

"It was pretty great," Bobby said. "Want to do it again?"

Laura peaked under the sheets to see Bobby was ready for round two.

"Oh, yes," she said. "Yes, I do."

They awoke the next morning after having scrambled eggs as a late-night dinner, then returned to the bedroom for more sex.

Bobby had gone in the kitchen and started coffee while Laura collected her clothing off the floor.

"You know you owe me a nice blouse," she said as she walked into the kitchen, her ripped blouse in her hand. "This one is ruined. Do you have any safety pins? I have to go back to the B&B and walk through the lobby."

"Don't want to do the walk of shame at the B&B?"

"I'd rather not, although today's my last day there. I have to move to a hotel for the next week."

"Well, wear one of my shirts back."

"You have a nice expensive shirt for me to wear?"

"You've seen what I wear. I have flannel shirts. Not that expensive."

"Do you have a favorite?"

"The one I wore yesterday," Bobby said, pointing to the plaid flannel shirt on the floor near the bedroom.

Laura picked it up and put it on, having trouble with the buttons that went opposite a woman's shirt.

"I'll expect that back," he said, worried.

"Of course," she said, smiling. "I'll be sure to return it in the same condition as my shirt."

"Hey, take it off then! I'll give you another shirt."

"Nope, I'll take this one. I'll give it back tomorrow. I've got to get back to the B&B and pack up."

"Where will you be?"

"Hampton Inn. Not that far away, but it's a step down from that lovely B&B."

"So, is it going to be weird between us now?" Bobby asked, handing Laura a cup of coffee.

"I can't imagine why it should. You still have your job to do and I have mine. But I'm certainly going to enjoy the friends with benefits aspect now."

"Are we friends?"

"Well, I hope so. I don't usually sleep with my enemies, do you?"

Bobby smiled wickedly. "No. And you were much better than Suzy. You were amazing."

"You are comparing me to Suzy?" Laura asked, her voice raising.

"I said you were better!"

"You are such an asshole," Laura said, wanting to throw her coffee cup at him. Instead, she slammed the coffee cup down on the counter and stormed out of Bobby's house. She walked briskly to the office, grabbed her handbag from inside, unlocked her car and sped out of the winery. Bobby looked on from his front door, coffee cup in hand, smiling.

Chapter 11

Laura drove fast back to the B&B, or as fast as her little 4-cylinder Chevrolet could go. She missed the throaty growl of her Mercedes-Benz with its Turbo. Her little rental had barely any get up and go.

As she pulled up to the B&B's parking area, she slammed the car door hard. Why did she let Bobby get to her like that? Just when she thought they might have a more amicable relationship, he says something to make her mad. Comparing her to Suzy! As if!

Laura now regretted sleeping with him. The act itself was incredible, which just made her angrier. She found it was a good stress reliever and she was feeling very stressed.

But she felt like Bobby had used her and she was unsure why, what his motives might have been. She didn't like that. Laura was the one who used men, not the other way around. Laura liked to be in control of her relationships. It made her feel safe.

Now she felt out of control with Bobby and that wasn't good. She worried about her work at the winery too. She worried she wouldn't be able to quantify the publicity when she next talked to Kyle Quitman.

She couldn't think about that right now. Now she needed to pack her belongings and move to the hotel. With her checkout time at the B&B and the hotel's check-in time gap, she'd have to find a place to work for about four hours. Laura wanted to do it at the winery office, but now thought that might not be a good idea.

Laura checked out of the B&B but set her laptop up at a small desk in its lobby. She grabbed another cup of coffee too. She didn't have breakfast at Bobby's and didn't think to stop at Starbucks on her way back for a breakfast treat. She was getting hungry.

She'd have to think about lunch soon, but she wanted to check in with Lee, the reporter Kimberly and send a few other emails.

By the time Laura looked up from her laptop it was close to one o'clock. She should probably pack up her laptop and grab lunch.

Then her cellphone rang. It was Bobby.

"What do you want?" Laura snapped as she answered.

"Well good afternoon to you, too, Laura. I was going to ask you to dinner, but maybe I'll call Suzy instead if you aren't interested."

"I didn't say I wasn't interested. And why would you call that tramp?"

"Careful. Pot calling the kettle black and all that."

"Are you calling me a tramp?" Laura shouted. She looked up and caught stares from other people in the lobby of the B&B and could see a desk clerk headed her way. She softened her tone. "I'd love to have dinner with you. What time are you picking me up?"

"Miss Lucas, I believe your reservation is up," the desk clerk said to her. She tried to grab Laura by the elbow to steer her out of the lobby, but Laura jerked her arm away.

"I'm on the phone, can't you see? I'll be leaving in just a moment."

"Who are you talking to?" Bobby asked.

"I'm being shown the door from the B&B. I've been using the lobby to get my work done."

"Why didn't you come here to the office?"

"I didn't think I was welcome," Laura said, collecting her jacket and laptop and moving toward the front door. The desk clerk followed her closely to make sure Laura left.

"Laura, you are welcome to work here in the office."

"Well, thanks. I'll just grab some lunch and be over. Can I grab you something or have you eaten?"

"You offering to bring me lunch?"

"If you are taking me to dinner tonight, the least I can do is bring you lunch."

"I'd really like a Big Mac, large fries with a large Coke," he said.

"Are you kidding me? You eat that junk?"

"Junk? It's delicious."

"Yuck. I'll pick it up for you. Maybe there is a healthier option for me."

"Healthy? Pick up a Big Mac for yourself. I bet you'll like it. I seem to remember you like to eat big meat."

Laura snorted, then laughed. "Touché. If I want a big piece of red meat, it will be a filet mignon, medium rare with blue cheese crumbles. And I want a dirty martini with it. In fact, I'd like that for dinner. Is there a Ruth's Chris near here?"

"I know a good steak house."

"OK. I'm in the car now, I'll have your Happy Meal to you soon," Laura hung up and started the Chevrolet. Even though she'd been mad at him earlier, she was looking forward to seeing Bobby and enjoying a good steak tonight. She hoped Bobby would be the dessert after the meal.

Laura pulled up to the office and got out with a McDonald's bag in hand. Bobby heard the car pull up and met her at the front door.

"Ah, you brought a meal for a champion!"

Laura handed over the bag. "A champion?"

Bobby leaned in close to Laura. "I didn't hear any complaints last night, so yeah, a champion."

Laura shook her head. "You didn't hear any complaints because you were sound asleep within two minutes."

Bobby arched an eyebrow. "You had complaints?"

Laura stood there trying to think of a sarcastic response when Bobby grabbed Laura around the waist, moving her toward his house. He threw his lunch bag on the ground as he kissed her.

"Let's make sure there are no complaints now."

Laura awoke entangled in Bobby's bedsheets. His leg was over one of hers and it was heavy. She tried to ease out from under his leg, but Bobby stirred and pulled her into him.

Laura could smell the musky scent of sex between them. The scent was arousing.

She saw Bobby smiling and could see he was awake.

"Why are you so happy?"

"Why shouldn't I be happy? I just had some nut clearing sex."

Laura rolled onto her left elbow, facing Bobby. "Nut clearing sex?"

"Yep, my nuts got emptied."

"I'd say that was crude, but then I'm hearing that from you."

"Are you saying I'm crude?"

"Crude, rude and totally nude. Just the way I like a man."

Bobby laughed out loud and pulled Laura to him. "Might be a little while before I can go again."

"How long is a little while?"

"If you are impatient, there must have been no complaints."

"I never said there was a complaint," Laura said, rolling onto her back.

Bobby's finger began to circle Laura's nipple.

"If you keep doing that, in a little while better be right now."

"You need to be patient."

Bobby leaned over and began to suck Laura's nipple. Then he ran his tongue around it.

Laura squirmed under the sheet.

"Bobby, you are making me hot."

"Good," he said. "Then my plan is working."

"You have a plan?"

"The plan works if you stop talking. From now on, you can't speak."

"No speaking? Is this some kind of joke?"

Bobby placed his finger over Laura's lips. She playfully bit his finger. He then wagged his finger at her, as if to say, no, no, no.

Bobby began to circle Laura's nipple again this time using his thumb. Laura's nipple became erect and Bobby used his thumbnail to scrape the sensitive skin across the top of it.

Laura gasped. "Bobby," she whispered.

"No talking," he replied. "Shhhh."

Bobby kept running his thumbnail over her nipple and Laura arched her back, aching for some sexual release. Laura was hoping this was arousing Bobby as well, but she couldn't tell. He gave no indication he was getting excited.

Laura tried to peak under the covers at Bobby's penis, but Bobby batted her hand away from the top sheet.

"You just need to relax," he said.

"I'm anything but relaxed," she replied.

"Shhhh. I said no talking."

Laura bit her lip. Bobby was still scraping his thumbnail across her nipple. It was almost becoming too sensitive and starting to hurt. But it was a good kind of hurt.

"Want me to go lower?" Bobby asked.

Laura just nodded as Bobby moved his hand down on her stomach, then lower to her pubic bone.

"Here?"

Laura nodded again, arching her back at him.

"Kitten, you keep moving your pussy toward me. Do you want my fingers in you?"

Laura nodded and groaned her assent.

Bobby began circling his fingers around her outer labia, then into her inner labia, then finally began circling her clit.

"Do you like this?"

Laura moaned with pleasure. She wanted to tell him what to do with his fingers and his tongue, but he'd told her not to speak. And for once, she was listening to a man's command.

"What about this?" Bobby said as he thrust his fingers forcefully inside her.

Laura gasped. Bobby was being a bit rough with her, but it felt good.

"You want a little more?" He whispered hoarsely in her ear.

Bobby's body was aligned with hers, but his fingers were deep inside her. She could feel how wet he was making her.

Bobby put three fingers inside her and began thrusting harder. He then spread his fingers as wide as he could. She could feel his fingernails scraping inside her.

Laura suddenly bucked her back in orgasm, fisting the bed sheets in her hands and shouting her pleasure.

"Did you like that?"

Laura could barely speak. In all of her sexual experience, she'd never had a man get her off like that. A low growl came from her throat.

"I take that as a yes," Bobby said.

"Yes," she whispered.

"Just buying a little time until I'm ready to take you again," he said.

Laura felt herself tingle with anticipation. She could hardly wait.

Laura awoke later that afternoon and sat up in the bed.

"What time is it?" She asked, shaking Bobby awake.

"Um, late afternoon?"

"How late afternoon? I'm supposed to check into my hotel today." She raised up on one elbow.

"Do you have to do that today? Can't you stay here tonight?" Bobby asked.

"If I don't check in, I'll lose my reservation. Help me find my clothes."

Laura put her feet on the floor and bent over to begin collecting her clothes by the bed. She found her thong, her bra and jeans, but had no idea where her blouse was.

"Where's my shirt? Help me find my shirt," she commanded. Laura had gone into her authoritative voice.

"Yes, ma'am," Bobby said, walking naked across the bedroom and scooping up Laura's blouse. "You looking for this?"

Laura snatched it out of his hand and began to put it on.

"I wish you wouldn't do that," Bobby said.

"Why not?"

"Because I'd like to take it all off of you."

"Bobby, be serious. I need to get my housing situation in order. I've got to have a place to stay."

Bobby was quiet for a moment, then said, "Stay here."

"Bobby, you can't be serious."

"I am serious. Don't check into a hotel. Stay here with me."

"Bobby, I appreciate what you are trying to do, but I need my space. I can't live here with you. I can't chance that you'll throw me out by tomorrow."

Bobby looked genuinely hurt. Laura walked over and kissed him deeply.

"I'm going to go check in to the hotel. I'll be back," she hesitated, then smiled. "Wait a minute. You owe me dinner. Why don't you pick me up, we'll have dinner and then break in the bed at my hotel. Maybe we'll even annoy the neighbors."

Then Bobby smiled. He slapped Laura's bottom playfully as she began to walk out the bedroom door. Laura turned to face him. Now it was Laura's turn to smile.

"Don't do that if you don't mean it."

Laura checked into the Hampton Inn, dropped her bags off in her room, then texted Bobby that she had arrived. She was hungry. She hadn't eaten her lunch. The smell of her wilted chicken salad was permeating her rental car all the way to the hotel.

Laura tried to grab a few of the chicken pieces off her salad as she drove to the hotel but they were cold and didn't taste good. She tossed it in the trash in the lobby as she waited to check in.

I'm all checked in, she texted Bobby. **Come get me for dinner.**

Laura waited for a response but got none. Annoyed, she texted: **Well, let me know.**

Laura unpacked her suitcase and then set up her laptop on the small desk in her room. She next unpacked her toiletries. She was correct in that the hotel didn't have a nice bathtub. In fact, hers was a narrow hotel-style tub that looked like it hadn't been cleaned in a while.

Laura heard her phone chime for a text message.

I've got chores to do before nightfall since I got nothing done today. Dinner might be later tonight. OK?

Laura smiled. Nothing done today. They certainly had done plenty that day, just not outside of the bedroom.

OK, she texted back.

True to his word, Bobby showed up at Laura's hotel at nine o'clock that night. Laura was ravenous. He drove them to a local steakhouse and Laura ordered a dirty martini and an appetizer for them to share.

Bobby ordered a glass of Cabernet.

When their drinks arrived, Laura and Bobby clinked glasses. Bobby took a sip.

"Not bad. Not as good as mine. But Sean King's winery isn't too bad."

"You know him?"

"I know everyone with a winery in Napa. Kind of a small club."

Laura took a large sip of her martini. She was pleased that the bartender had remembered the blue cheese stuffed olives she'd asked for. It looked like he'd hand stuffed them with real blue cheese, not the jarred olives with crappy blue cheese from the store.

The dirty martini went straight to her head but was relaxing her. She wouldn't order another. Maybe she'd get a Cabernet with her meal.

"Bobby, what is your biggest concern about the winery?"

"What do you mean? I'm concerned about getting a good harvest. I'm concerned about disease on the grapes."

"And both of those things are out of your control, right?"

"By and large, yes. I have to have the right amount of rain, the right amount of sun for a good harvest."

"What about for the disease? How do you try to control that?"

"Sometimes I have to spray the vines, but I really don't like to. It's expensive. I'd rather cut the vines and cut my losses. The other fear is fire."

"Fire? Does that happen a lot?"

"More than we'd all like in California. The dry Santa Ana winds create a fire danger. Lightning, fireworks, and carelessness all cause bad fires here."

"God, that's terrible. Has Star 1 ever burned?"

"We've had a few fires. Small ones. We got them out quickly."

"I'm sure that was a relief."

"It would be devastating if that happened on a large scale."

Bobby and Laura were silent for a moment. Laura hadn't meant for the conversation to turn dark. Bobby seemed to be lost in his thoughts. Then he smiled.

"What are you doing over the weekend?" Bobby asked. "Are you working on publicity stuff or are you taking weekends off?"

"I'll be working some of tomorrow. Why?"

"I've got to drive down to San Francisco and wanted to see if you'd like to come with me."

"Is it far?"

"About an hour, hour and a half, depending on what kind of traffic we hit."

"What time are you planning to leave tomorrow?" Laura asked.

"I'd like to get an early start, maybe at eight. I've got to meet a guy about distribution for next year. Told him I'd meet him around 10:30. Then we could have the day to tour the city. Have you ever been to San Francisco?"

"Never. This is my first time to the west coast. I've spent most of my time on the east coast. Miami, Virginia, New York City, of course, and Atlanta. And a few smaller cities in between when I had work to do for clients."

"So, you'd like to come with me tomorrow?"

"I'd love to. And I bet you will make the perfect tour guide."

"You know, if you spent the night, we could leave right on time," Bobby said with a smile.

"Oh, really now? Well, I'd better grab a small overnight bag when you take me back to the hotel."

Chapter 12

For the second morning in a row, Laura awoke in Bobby's arms. She rolled over to face him.

"Good morning, lover," she said, softly.

"Good morning to you. Did you sleep well?"

"I always sleep well after great sex."

"Still no complaints, huh?"

"No complaints at all."

"Did you pack comfortable shoes for today?"

"I have some sandals," Laura replied.

"Are they flats?"

"No, they are heels. Why?"

"San Francisco is meant to be walked. You don't have any athletic shoes with a rubber sole?"

"Not on this trip."

"Well, you can certainly try walking in your shoes, but don't blame me if you have blisters later or if you are begging me to stop to buy new shoes."

"I'll be fine."

Bobby looked skeptically at Laura. "OK. They are your feet. You should have brought your boots."

"Do I have time for a shower?"

"Can you be quick about it? We need to get on the road soon."

"I'll be quick. Do you have a hair dryer?"

Bobby shook his head no. "I am not the Hampton Inn."

"Well, then, no shower until we get back. My hair would stay wet until we got there, I'm sure."

"It is nice and thick," Bobby said, running his fingers through Laura's black hair. "And it smells nice, like a pina colada."

"My shampoo smells like coconut."

"Yeah, like I said, a pina colada."

"I didn't take you for a fruity rum cocktail drinker."

"I was in high school. I drank just about anything I could get my hands on back then. Didn't you?"

"I went to a Catholic high school," Laura responded.

"And you were a good Catholic girl who only drank the communion wine?"

"It was grape juice at my church," Laura laughed at the memory. "I think the priests were the only ones drinking the real stuff. Vin Santo and all that. From grape juice to fine wine, my tastes have certainly evolved."

"OK, get dressed. We need to get on the road. We can talk about your evolved tastes in my truck."

"We should have come back from my hotel in my rental car."

"No, my truck will be fine."

Laura wasn't so sure she wanted to ride all the way to San Francisco in Bobby's work truck.

Bobby held a travel cup of coffee out to Laura. "We'll grab a late breakfast in San Francisco. I know a great bakery." Then he looked down at her stylish sandals. He thought the heels were way too high to be comfortable walking in San Francisco.

"I think you are going to regret your footwear today. I plan on being a real tour guide and walking to Fisherman's Wharf and through Chinatown. You are going to see as much of the sights as you can in one day."

"What about the Golden Gate Bridge?"

"If it's not fogged in you should be able to see it."

"I've only ever seen pictures of it. I'm excited to see the real thing."

Bobby walked around to the passenger side door and opened it for Laura.

"A real gentleman," she remarked.

"My mother raised me right."

He climbed into the driver's side and started the truck and pulled away from the winery on the way to San Francisco.

They got to the edge of the city and Bobby pulled off the highway and into a suburb. He parked the truck outside of a small Chinese bakery.

"They have some of the best baked goods here," he said, locking the truck.

They entered the small store and Laura could smell fresh brewed coffee and sweet pastries. Her mouth began to water.

Bobby and Laura stood in line waiting to order at the counter. When they stepped up Bobby ordered four mooncakes and two coffees. Laura started to order, but Bobby cut her off.

"Trust me, you'll love these mooncakes. You'll thank me later."

Laura pouted because she had her eye on a cream-filled pastry, but she stopped herself as the clerk handed over two coffees to her. Bobby paid for their goods, grabbed the bakery bag and began looking for a table to sit and eat.

Another couple was leaving a small bistro table and Bobby and Laura claimed it. Laura stood and said she was going to fix her coffee. Bobby nodded since he liked his black.

Laura returned and Bobby had already eaten one of the mooncakes. "Couldn't wait?"

"You'll understand when you eat one," he said, wiping his mouth on a white paper napkin.

Laura took a small bite of the mooncake and realized Bobby was right. The mooncake was delicious. The dense cake was sweet and salty and completely satisfying. She was glad he'd bought four of them.

Bobby was stuffing the last of his in his mouth as Laura started her second one.

"They're good, aren't they?" Bobby asked. Laura could only nod since her mouth was full.

Bobby crunched up the paper bag and stood up to toss it in the trash bin. He grabbed his coffee. Laura was still sipping her coffee but looked up to see Bobby scowl at her.

"Sorry, we can't linger. Got to make my appointment at 10:30."

He held the door of the bakery for her, then went around to the door of his truck for her. He went around to the driver's side and started the truck.

"You know you don't have to open my truck door every time," Laura said when Bobby pulled away from the bakery. "I mean it's nice, but if you are in a hurry to get to your appointment, you don't have to do it."

"We're fine for time, I think. I just never know what the traffic will be like getting into the city."

"Don't you have Waze to tell you what the traffic is like?"

"Waze?"

"It's this traffic app that lets you know if there are wrecks ahead and all that. It's indispensable in Atlanta. There's always something crazy going on with traffic. Did you know there was a zebra loose on one of our major highways a few years ago? It made the national news."

"A zebra? How the hell did that happen? Was the circus in town or something?"

"Hell if I know, but it created traffic chaos."

"I bet."

"Download the Waze app and it will tell you what the traffic is like next time you come down here."

"I really don't need that. I've made this trip plenty of times. I know what the traffic can be like."

As they neared the next exit, traffic slowed to a stop. Laura looked over at Bobby and sighed heavily.

She reached into her purse and pulled out her phone. "What's the address where we're going?"

Bobby gave her the address, Laura punched it into her Waze app and saw there was "police activity" ahead.

"What does police activity mean?"

"In Atlanta it means there's probably been a drive-by shooting on the highway and police are there, blocking the lanes, to investigate."

"Will your app tell me how to get around this?"

Laura nodded. "See if you can get over and exit at this next exit. Waze will reroute us."

Bobby put his turn signal on and eased over into the right lane and made the exit. Laura's phone then began giving directions to get around the problem.

There were a few left turns, a couple of right turns down a smaller highway with plenty of traffic lights, but eventually they were back on the highway.

"That was helpful. Thanks," he said.

"Told you. We should be getting there right about 10:30, maybe just a few minutes after. Do you need to call your guy and let him know you'll be late?"

"No, he'll wait."

Bobby parked his truck in front of a small brick office building.

"Do you mind waiting in the truck? I won't be that long, maybe a half hour. If I'm longer, I'll come out and let you know."

"Trade secrets I can't know about?" Laura teased.

"Something like that."

"I'll be fine. Leave me the keys so I can turn on the air conditioner if I get warm."

"It's not even going to be 65 degrees today," Bobby said. "You might need the heat before you need the air conditioner."

"Well with the windows up it might get stuffy. Just leave me the keys, please. I promise I won't go joyriding in your truck."

Bobby tossed the keys to Laura and went into the building.

Bobby returned to the truck about 45 minutes later. "Sorry, we had more to talk about than I thought," he said as he got in.

"No problem. So, you have a new distributor?"

Bobby looked at Laura puzzled. "What?"

"You said you were meeting this guy for wine distribution, right?"

"Oh, right," Bobby said. "Yeah, this guy owes me a favor."

Laura looked at Bobby. She thought he was being evasive, but she didn't know why. Was this man a new distributor, or wasn't he? And if he wasn't, why was Bobby being so secretive? She wondered if he didn't want her in the meeting because he didn't want her to know what this 'favor' was.

"Now, are you ready for the grand tour of San Francisco?"

Laura nodded. She was excited to see the sites.

Bobby had parked his truck in a garage near Chinatown. Then they had started walking down Grant Avenue from the Dragon Gate. They stopped for a late lunch at a restaurant, before catching the Powell-Hyde cable car to Fisherman's Wharf. They could see the Golden Gate Bridge and could see Alcatraz in the distance.

By the time Laura got back into Bobby's truck, she took her sandals off. The blisters on her feet were bleeding. She quickly put some bandages on her heels and on two of her toes. She then gently put her sandals back on, but she didn't strap them on. She kept them loose on her feet.

"I tried to tell you," Bobby said.

"Shut up."

"Don't get mad at me."

"I'm mad at you and myself."

"Why me?"

"You could have told me to pack my boots for today. They've got a lower heel. My God my back is killing me."

"But did you have fun today?"

"You were a great tour guide. I just need to cut my feet off at my ankles. Do you have any ibuprofen?"

"Check the glove box."

Laura opened the truck's glove box and pulled out old napkins, receipts, a flashlight and a few tools. "I don't see anything in here, except your junk."

"Should be a small white bottle in there," he said pointing in the direction of the open glove box. Bobby was trying to concentrate on turning out of the parking deck and merging into late afternoon traffic.

Laura rummaged through the glove box again and pulled the bottle out. She opened it and popped four pills in her mouth. She had to dry swallow them and winced as they went down.

"Hell, how many did you take?" Bobby asked, alarmed.

"Four. That's prescription strength."

"Do you need prescription strength?"

"Both my feet hurt, my back hurts and I have a headache. So, yes, I need prescription strength," she snapped.

"Don't bite my head off, I just asked."

"You were judging me."

"Fine. Take prescription strength if you need it."

"I do need it."

Bobby and Laura did not speak again until they were nearly back at the winery, except Bobby didn't turn into the winery.

"Where are you going?" Laura asked.

"I'm dropping you off at your hotel."

Laura said nothing. When he stopped at the Hampton Inn, Laura grabbed her bag, took off her sandals and jumped out of the truck, slamming the door behind her.

Bobby stood halfway out of his truck. "You're welcome," he shouted at her back.

Laura turned and flipped him off. Then she walked into the hotel, hearing the automatic doors closing behind her.

When she got to her room, she got a washcloth and soap and scrubbed out the bathtub as best she could. She desperately wanted to soak in the tub to ease her feet and her back. She ran the water as hot as she could get it, but it really turned out just a little too warm.

She stripped down and eased her feet in. It was painful, so she quickly sat down and put her feet on the edges of the tub and out of the water. The tub was much smaller than the one at the B&B, so she had to bend her knees to get her shoulders into the water.

She wished she'd thought to bring a glass of wine into the tub with her, but the warm water was starting to relax her.

Laura could not believe how Bobby acted on the drive home, giving her the silent treatment. He should have told her the night before to pack more sensible shoes. But she loved those sandals. It was not her fault she had blisters to deal with now.

Bobby was such an asshole, Laura thought. An asshole that she really enjoyed screwing. And that just made her madder.

The bathwater had turned cold. Laura got out, toweled off and poured a glass of wine into the small drinking glass in her room. She should think about dinner. She should think about liberating another bottle of Cabernet from Star 1 if she got the chance. Instead, she took a few sips of the wine, slipped under the covers and fell into an exhausted sleep.

Chapter 13

Laura was so exhausted from the walking tour of San Francisco she slept later than she expected. She got up quickly, tossed on some clothes put on a pair of socks on her blistered feet and just managed to make it downstairs for breakfast at the hotel before the staff cleared it away.

There wasn't much left. She only had a few scrambled eggs, some breakfast sausages that had been under the heat lamps a little too long, coffee and toast.

Laura was really missing the B&B's breakfasts. The three-egg omelet, the French toast and the spinach and mushroom frittatas were a delightful memory now. But she dared not complain, since she hadn't had dinner last night. She grabbed an apple from the basket after she refilled her coffee cup and took the elevator back to her room.

Laura showered and dressed casually for the day. She expected she'd be working in her room all day. Since she'd had that fight with Bobby, she didn't want to go to the office.

She wore jeans, a long-sleeved dark green cotton blouse and kept her sore feet bare. That was another reason she decided to stay put in her room that day. With her feet still blistered, she didn't think she could bear to put on a pair of shoes, even her more comfortable boots.

By early afternoon, Laura realized she was getting hungry. She'd have to run out for something to eat. Maybe she'd put on several bandages and take a chance by wearing her high-heeled sandals once again to eat at a nice cafe.

Laura parked at a nearby cafe and was surprised to see Lee's truck there.

She entered the cafe and saw Lee sitting at a table talking to another gentleman. Laura walked gingerly over to their table and said hello.

"Laura," Lee said, standing up. "So good to see you. This is my friend Brent Jones. Brent, this is Laura Lucas."

Brent stood up and shook Laura's hand. They made pleasant greeting noises to each other.

"Laura, I'm glad I ran into you. I've got the video of the winery back at my place. Are you free this afternoon to come over to look at it?"

"Sure, I've got your address," she replied.

"Would you like to join us?" Brent asked, looking around to find a chair to pull up.

"No, no. I see you are finishing your meals. What time would you like me to meet you, Lee?"

"How about three o'clock?"

"I'll see you at three. Nice meeting you, Brent."

Laura got a small table near the window of the cafe and ordered. The bright sunshine almost made her reach for her sunglasses in her bag, but instead she switched her seat so the sun was to her back, warming it so that she needed to take off her jacket.

She ended up getting two starters, a mixed-greens salad and a stuffed portobello mushroom. Laura almost couldn't finish her meal.

She paid for her meal and looked at her watch. It was not quite two o'clock. Laura would need to find something to kill an hour before heading to Lee's house. She drove to downtown Napa and parked and window shopped at some of the boutique stores. Laura went in a couple of them but was becoming mindful of how much money she had already spent on this trip.

The food alone was so expensive. She'd planned to expense everything, but what if Kyle Quitman decided the expenses she turned in would come out of her share of the money she made him?

Even though she found a lovely burgundy scarf that would look great with her coloring, Laura put it back. The salesclerk tried to flatter her into buying it, but Laura knew those tricks, too. She left the scarf in the store.

By the time she got back to her rental car, it was slightly after three o'clock. She called Lee before she backed out of her parking space and told him she was on her way.

Laura turned up the short driveway of Lee Adams' small light gray bungalow house. Lee was at the front door waiting for her, ready to usher her inside.

"I hope you found it OK," he said.

"I was glad for my phone's GPS. There were a few turns I missed on my way here."

"Sorry about that."

"No, it's fine. I hope I am not keeping you from another client appointment."

"My dear, you are my only one for this afternoon. Can I get you something to drink? I've got a nice buttery Chardonnay. Can I interest you in a glass? And please say yes. I hate to drink alone."

Laura said she'd be delighted to have a glass of white wine.

Lee showed Laura into his video suite and disappeared into his kitchen to get the wine. When he returned to the room, he had the wine glasses on a tray, along with the wine bottle in a chiller and some cheese and crackers on a small plate.

"I brought us some snacks as well," he said, putting the tray down on a nearby table by the chairs in front of the computer. "You can tell I tend to live in this room. Behind that door is my dark room," he said, nodding his head toward a closed door.

"Dark room? You still shoot with film? I thought everything was digital these days," she remarked.

"There is just something about film. I like to play with film and filters every now and again. Therefore, a dark room."

"I'm excited to see the video."

"I've got a contact sheet from the photo shoots, too. Let me grab that." Lee got up and ruffled through a stack of papers on the corner of a large desk behind the computer. He pulled out several sheets of paper with small photos on them. As he handed the papers to Laura, he also offered her a magnifier loupe.

Laura put the loupe to her eye and bent toward the first contact sheet.

"Oh, I like these. Can I mark up the ones I really like? The ones I think I'd like for the website whenever I can get admin privileges?"

"You still don't have those? Did you call my guy?"

"Sorry, I got distracted yesterday. Took a day trip up to San Francisco with Bobby. I'll call your guy tomorrow."

"You get along with Bobby?"

"Sometimes yes, sometimes no."

"I was a little worried when you wanted me for this gig. Bobby's got a bit of a reputation."

"Reputation? What do you mean?"

"He's made some enemies in the vintner community. He can be, how shall I put it...."

"An asshole?" Laura interjected.

"Why yes, an asshole," Lee said, smiling broadly at the thought.

"What did he do to make enemies?" she asked.

"Well, what didn't he do? Are you sure you want me to talk about your boss? Some of it's not so nice."

"He's not my boss. I work for the investor who now owns his winery."

"And that's one thing that has put him in bad light with some of the other vintners. He sold out to the highest bidder. Vintners are proud to be small, independent wine makers. Selling out to an investor did not sit well with many of them."

"From what I can see he was not happy to sell and he's not rolling in money."

"That's not what some of the other vintners say. They say he got paid lots for a winery that needs work by some greenhorn who didn't know what he was buying. And the investor left the one man who can't run it right in charge of it."

Laura was quiet.

"I'm sorry. I shouldn't be bad mouthing Bobby, especially since you have to work with him."

"No, I appreciate your candor. Knowledge is power, right? Anything else I should know about?"

"Well, and this is just a rumor, and you did not hear it from me because I'll deny it, but Bobby's supposed to be dealing with some shady people these days."

"Shady people? What kind of shady people?"

"People who are doing him favors. Dangerous favors."

"What do you mean by that?"

"I shouldn't have said anything. Just be careful around him, Laura. You seem like a lovely woman and I wouldn't want you to get caught up in anything criminal."

Laura's eyebrows shot up with surprise. "Criminal!"

"Well, if not criminal, just a little below the law."

"I really don't understand."

"And I can't explain it more than that. Would you like another glass of wine? Then I want to show you the video. The drone footage is awesome if I do say so myself."

Lee walked over and got the bottle of Chardonnay, poured Laura and himself another glass, then returned the bottle to the chiller.

"This is really delicious," Laura said, holding the glass up to look at the golden liquid.

"Have more. I have another bottle chilling in my wine cellar."

Lee and Laura watched the video. Laura took notes and made some suggestions on what she liked and what she didn't necessarily like. She thought the video ought to be no more than 60 seconds, because she wanted it on Star 1's landing page. But she also wanted smaller videos that could be embedded on other pages.

Lee said he thought he could make a slideshow of the various bottles of wine and intersperse some of the shots of models looking happy.

Laura liked that idea. She picked out some of the models and photos she'd like to include. None of them included Suzy.

Afternoon turned to early evening and Laura and Lee had moved out of the video suite and into Lee's living room. He opened another bottle of Chardonnay and offered her a light supper.

"I have more cheese, some really nice baguettes, strawberries, dates and some sausages. We can have a pauper's meal."

"That sounds lovely. I had such a late lunch that a light supper would be perfect. But I don't want to put you out. I can go."

"Oh no, please. I need to eat, too. Please stay and be my guest. I hate eating alone and unfortunately I do it quite often."

"Well, if you insist," she teased.

"I do."

Lee got out a serving platter and sliced some summer sausages, more cheese, the bread and gathered some dates, fruit and olives. He also put more crackers on the platter. He poured each of them another glass from the new wine bottle.

He directed Laura to sit on the sofa and he sat on the other end.

"Oh, I don't want to spill on your sofa," Laura said. "Can't we sit at the table?"

"It's more comfortable here on the sofa. I tend to eat here all the time. And I know you won't spill."

"I'm glad you have faith in me."

"I have every faith in you, my dear. Tell me a little more about yourself, Laura. Why are you here in Napa?"

"I told you part of it. I work in marketing and PR back in Atlanta. I have my own business like you. I got hired by Kyle Quitman, the investor who bought Star 1, to get some actionable publicity for the winery."

"What do you mean by 'actionable publicity'?"

"I mean I have to create real dollars and cents, a measurable tick in income, or I don't get paid."

"That sounds like a lousy deal."

"It is. I never should have agreed to it, but I need the money. You know how it is. One day you are rolling in clients and can pay the bills, and the next day, poof, you can't."

Lee nodded his head. He did know what being a self-employed photographer was like. Only Laura never had to deal with bridezillas, and he told her that.

Laura laughed out loud. "Well, you've got me there. My clients were mostly in commercial real estate. I do have to deal with larger-than-life egos, but not an outraged bride."

"Oh, the stories I could tell you," he said, reaching out to refill Laura's wine glass.

"This has to be the last one, Lee. I've got to drive back to my hotel."

"No, you don't, Laura. You could stay the night if you want."

Laura looked at Lee. Did he expect her to sleep with him?

"Lee, I don't think that's a good idea."

"Why not? I'm lonely. You are lonely."

"Lee, in this case I don't want to mix business with pleasure. I've had a lovely evening, but I think I should go."

"Is it because you are seeing Bobby?"

Laura was surprised. "No. It's not that at all," she lied, standing up. She didn't want to look at Lee in case her expression gave her away.

Lee stood up as well, moving to embrace her. Laura kept him at arm's length but allowed him to give her a small kiss. Lee tried to kiss her again. Laura put her arm out and gave him a slight push.

"Lee, please don't make this difficult. I do like you and I want to continue to work with you, as professionals."

"Well, you can't blame me for trying. You are a beautiful woman, Laura."

"Thank you, Lee. Now good night."

Laura drove back to her hotel deep in thought. She didn't find Lee Adams unattractive at all. It's just having slept with Bobby, she decided she didn't want to complicate her life further. She wondered what was happening to her. In her younger years she had no qualms about sleeping with her clients, especially one as attractive as Lee.

Maybe she was maturing. She gave a slight shudder at the thought. Laura nearly turned the car around to head back to Lee's house. Then she thought better of the idea.

Laura pulled into the hotel's parking lot and realized she'd missed a call from Bobby.

Now what, she thought to herself.

What do you want? she fired off an angry text.

Moments later her cell rang, the call from Bobby.

"Well, that message doesn't sound very friendly."

"You are trying my patience these days, Bobby."

"How are your feet?"

"Still blistered."

"Want to come over? I can give you a soothing foot massage."

Laura's panties got damp at the thought.

"Just my feet?"

"I can massage anything of yours that might need soothing."

"I'll be there in a few minutes."

Laura started her car and began to head immediately out of the parking lot. Then she stopped and thought about going up to her room and grabbing a change of clothes.

She parked, took the elevator to her floor and quickly grabbed a few clothes, stuffing them in a plastic shopping bag, and then headed back to her car. Laura was not doing the walk of shame through the hotel lobby tomorrow morning.

Laura arrived at the winery at nearly ten o'clock at night. The air smelled fresh and damp as she stepped out of her car.

Bobby stood at the front door of his home.

"That didn't take long," he said.

"I was in my car when you called."

"Where've you been?"

"I was at Lee Adams' house. We were going over the video he shot and I looked at the contact sheets for the photos. They are very good."

"At this time of night?" Bobby asked, an eyebrow raised.

"Don't get all excited. When we were done looking at everything, he served me some wine and a light supper."

"Is that all he served you?"

"Don't be crude. He's harmless."

"Harmless? He's been accused of, shall we say, unwanted attention toward the ladies."

"You mean he assaulted someone? A woman?"

"Don't think it went that far, and he was never charged, but the word around Napa is he is a bit of a playboy or plays himself off as one. I'd be careful around him if I were you. That's why I was surprised you hired him. Of course, you wouldn't know that, not being from here."

Laura was surprised and she would be more careful around him. She was glad nothing had happened between them earlier in the evening.

"Well, I was promised a foot massage, among other things," Laura said, changing the subject.

"I can make that happen," he said, closing the bedroom door behind them.

Chapter 14

Laura felt Bobby stir next to her in his king-sized bed, which took up nearly the whole bedroom.

Groggy from sleep, she asked, "What time is it?"

"It's five in the morning."

"What are you doing getting up?"

"I get up most mornings this early, when I'm not distracted by a beautiful woman. I've got some chores to do. I told you this is essentially a working farm."

"But you don't have to feed the cows or anything. Come back to bed," she pleaded.

"Sorry, I can't. I'll make some coffee so you'll have that when you get up," Bobby said, bending to kiss Laura on the lips.

Laura flopped back down on the pillow and pulled the warm covers over her naked body. She had nearly fallen back asleep when she heard a loud engine start up. It sounded like a truck, and it sounded like it was right near Bobby's house. She pulled the pillow over her head to try to block out the sound.

As the winery began to come alive, she could hear men's voices talking loudly over the engines and motors of different vehicles.

Laura sighed and pulled the pillow off her head. She'd never get back to sleep now. She got up, dressed in her new clothes, found the discarded clothing from the night before strewn about the bedroom and stuffed those back in her plastic bag.

She stepped out into the small kitchen, found a coffee cup that looked clean and poured the dark rich liquid in it. She managed to find some sugar and poured a lot of it into her coffee.

Laura decided she'd be better off back at her hotel, where she could get some sleep and then some breakfast. She found a scrap of paper in her handbag and then a pen, scratching out a note that she'd gone back to the hotel.

Laura tucked the note under her now empty coffee cup on the counter and left.

Once back at the hotel, Laura crawled into her unmade hotel bed, setting her phone's alarm for a more reasonable wake up time of eight o'clock. She felt like she'd just gotten back to sleep when her alarm sounded. She roused herself, showered, dressed and went down to the breakfast area to eat.

Today's choice was a slightly watery omelet with cheese, some breakfast links, and toast. She expected to email Kyle later that morning with a report on her progress.

She hoped with what she'd put in motion, she could show she was working to get publicity for the winery. She also wanted to call Lee's contact about the website. If Laura could get that squared away, she could really show Kyle her efforts.

After her emails to Kyle and a few follow ups to several magazine editors and local reporters, she emailed Kimberly to see when the feature on the winery would run.

Kimberly shot back an email to say her editor had moved the feature up, and it was scheduled to run in the next issue.

Laura asked if Kimberly needed any more photos and asked if she'd be allowed to read the feature before it ran. Laura knew very well that most publications did not allow pre-publication review, but she always asked. She was in PR after all. She wanted to control the story and how the winery was portrayed.

Kimberly responded with a polite email that said Laura would not be allowed to read it before it was published. Blah blah blah, Laura thought.

Laura thanked Kimberly for the opportunity to feature Star 1, then she put away her laptop. She picked up her cellphone to call Bobby.

"Hey," he said. "I got home and you weren't here."

"I didn't realize how noisy it would be. I came back to the hotel to get more sleep."

"Well, I'm sorry you weren't here. I was ready for another round of massages."

"Oh, you were, were you?"

"And you weren't here. I couldn't give you another massage."

"And I couldn't give you another blowjob."

"Well, who's fault is that?"

"Tell your workers to keep the tractor noise down and I'd have been there."

"Ha! Not going to happen. Sorry."

"Well, you could always stay at my hotel tonight. We wouldn't be disturbed."

"I'd still have to get up early to get back to the winery."

"That's no fun."

"Are you coming back to the winery today?"

"I plan to come back later this afternoon," she said.

"I'll take some steaks out of the freezer. I can put those on the grill tonight."

"Sounds good. I'll see you later today."

"OK. See you then."

Bobby had the coals going on his outdoor grill. He even threw some hickory chips on them to give the steaks a bit of flavor. When he thought the coals were hot enough, he put the thick cut ribeye steaks on the grill.

Bobby had opened a bottle of Cabernet Sauvignon reserve and put it in a wide-bottomed decanter to allow the wine to breathe.

"Can I help?" Laura asked as Bobby moved around his small kitchen, putting some potatoes out of the oven and getting some spinach ready to sauté.

"You can keep me company," he replied.

"Is this going to be as good as the steakhouse you took me to?"

"It will be better," he answered.

"That's some tall talk."

"It's the truth. I have my own special marinade. It makes the steaks taste better."

"OK. You're the chef, and the winemaker. You certainly are a man of many talents."

"I hope to show you a few more of my talents tonight after dinner."

"Oooh, I'd like that."

"I thought you would."

"I talked to that guy Lee knows, the one who can help us with the website."

"And what did he say?"

"He said he'll work on getting the admin privileges back and assigned to you," she said.

"Oh no. I don't want that responsibility. Why don't you do it?"

"Well, I won't be here forever. You need to decide who in the company can update the website. Don't you have a young guy who likes that techy stuff? And could upload new photos and other media every now and again?"

"I'll have to think about it. There is one guy who is a big gamer. Into those online video games and all. Maybe he could do it. He might understand it."

"Well, let me talk to him to see if he really is capable of running the website. I'm not saying he can't. I'll also ask Kyle if I can do it for you. Then you'd really be a client for me. That would maybe mean he has to hire me."

Bobby pulled the steaks off the grill and got them onto the plates. He pulled baked potatoes out of the oven and grabbed a bag of spinach that he threw into a hot pan with olive oil and garlic.

"You certainly know your way around the kitchen. My panties are getting wet," Laura teased.

Bobby put the sauteed spinach on the plates next to the other food.

"Good to know," Bobby said, putting the plates on the table. "So, you want to be hired by him? Kyle Quitman, I mean?"

"I need some new clients. And If he'll hire me, I bet I can do a lot of publicity work for his various businesses. My mortgage isn't going to pay itself, Bobby."

"It never does. I just don't understand why you'd want to work for that guy. He's married, you know."

"I know that."

"His wife is very nice. She came out to the winery with him right before he bought me out."

"But he left you to keep running Star 1. He must have faith in you."

Bobby shrugged his shoulders. "Faith," he laughed. Then his tone turned bitter. "I just think he doesn't want to get his hands dirty with the winery. He doesn't strike me as a man who ever gets his hands dirty. I'm just the hired help and I like to get my hands dirty."

"Clearly you love what you do, or you wouldn't be doing it," she said.

"I do love what I do. I just wish I was still doing it for me. Not for him. If only I hadn't gotten so behind with the bank. Quitman came with an offer I really could not refuse. I was going to lose the winery. And there were plenty of sharks circling the water to buy me out."

"What do you mean?"

"There are plenty of vintners around here who would love to see me fail – Sean King being one of them – and buy this place to expand their own vineyards. With Quitman's offer, now they can't. At least not for a while."

"What happens if Kyle ever decides he wants to sell or to get out?"

"I'd better be able to buy the winery back, or I'm screwed."

"Can you buy it back?"

"Not yet. I've got to get my finances in order and get my credit score up. So, I hope Quitman holds on to it for a while."

"I hope for your sake that happens."

Bobby and Laura finished their steaks. Laura said it was as good, if not better than the steakhouse Bobby had taken her to a few nights before. They had the bottle of the Cabernet Sauvignon reserve, which Laura loved. The taste on her tongue was exquisite.

"Hey, I meant to tell you earlier. That feature on Star 1 got moved up. It is now scheduled for the next issue in a couple of weeks. I got an email from Kimberly today."

"That's good, right?" Bobby asked.

"That's great. That's what Kyle wants. This is the very first deliverable I have to send him, until the website gets fixed."

They moved into the living room and Bobby started a fire in the fireplace. The Napa nights could be chilly in early June. Bobby pulled a lap blanket out and draped it over Laura.

"Did you bring an overnight bag?" he asked.

"Is the pope Catholic?" she quipped.

"Well, you'd know that better than me."

"What religion are you, Bobby?"

"I don't have one. My mother used to make us go to church as a kid, but once I was grown, I never went again."

"I don't go anymore either."

The pair got quiet as the flames licked the wood in the fireplace. Laura put her head on Bobby's shoulder as he circled his fingers around her left knee.

"This is nice," she said. "Who knew I'd go for a quiet evening in?"

"This is me every night."

"I could almost get used to it. It's so peaceful here. In Atlanta, I can hear car traffic at night, and I'm up in the penthouse. Occasionally I can hear gunfire too."

"Gunfire? What kind of city are you living in?"

"One where there is lots of street noise and occasional gunfire."

"I don't think I could give up this quiet for a noisy city."

They were quiet again. Laura could hear an owl hooting.

"There's a noise I never hear in Atlanta," she said.

"What noise?"

"That owl. Sounds pretty close."

"Probably not that close and probably catching mice out in the vineyard. They are good to have around."

"Are there other wildlife out here?"

"Racoons, deer, fox. Occasionally a bobcat. Every now and again there are sightings of bear and mountain lions."

"Oh God! We certainly don't have those in Atlanta."

"Just zebra, right?"

Laura laughed. "Yeah, just the occasional runaway zebra."

Bobby laughed too. "Should I put more wood on the fire, or should we head to bed?"

"I'm nice and cozy by the fire, but I know I'll be nice and cozy in the bed next to you, too," she said.

"Bed it is. I'll let the fire die out then," Bobby said, standing up and poking the wood with a fire poker to make the wood level. He then returned the metal screen in front of the fireplace.

Laura stood up, wrapping the blanket around her. Bobby helped steer her into the bedroom, then unwrapped the blanket around her body.

"I'm chilly," Laura admitted.

"I'll be sure to warm you up."

Laura emitted a quick squeal. And Bobby emitted a low growl.

They fell onto the king-sized bed, devouring each other with kisses. Eventually, their clothes became strewn across the bedroom.

Laura could not contain her cries of ecstasy when she came. Bobby fell on top of her after he was spent.

They both tried to catch their breath after they were sexually satisfied. Laura felt she and Bobby were so in sync sexually. She nuzzled into his shoulder and began to hear his breathing slowly get even. Then she heard his soft snores. Laura wasn't far behind in slumber.

Bobby shook Laura violently. "Laura! Laura! Wake up! You're having a bad dream!"

Laura had thrashed and kicked in her sleep, crying out, "No, Julio! Stop! Stop it!"

Laura sat up with a start. Her heart was racing. "What? What's happening?"

"You were having a bad dream," Bobby said softly. "Who is Julio? You kept saying his name."

Laura paused, confused. "Julio?"

"You kept shouting for him to stop. Stop what, Laura?"

Laura put her face in her hands. She was quiet for a moment then whispered, "Oh, God, Bobby. He was an ex-boyfriend when I was much younger. He assaulted me — hit me. I have bad dreams about him sometimes."

Laura was not going to tell Bobby Julio had done much worse than hit her.

Even in the dim night light, Laura could see Bobby's face cloud over. "Jesus! He hit you? I'd like to break his neck. No man should ever hit a woman."

"I agree. I'm sorry I woke you."

"No, no. It's OK. You don't still run into him, do you?"

"No, he's dead."

"Dead?"

"Got shot in gang warfare."

"He was in a gang?"

"He was. It was a long time ago, Bobby. I shouldn't have been dating him. I regret that I ever got involved with him."

Bobby pulled Laura to him in the dark. "You are safe with me, baby doll. You are safe with me I'll never hurt you that way."

"I know."

A dark figure moved through the vines on the far end of the winery. He was hidden well in the shadows but knew the rows well.

He could see his breath in the cool night air. The shadowy figure wore dark sleeves and pants, so he was sure he couldn't be seen, but he also was sweating, his heart racing as he splashed gasoline along the long rows of vines.

He walked what he thought was about a quarter mile, then crossed through the vines and began on the other side, soaking budding grapes and vines in gasoline. When the 10-gallon gas can was empty, the figure went to the spot where he'd left the other 10-gallon can. He walked back up the row from the opposite end.

He got his final 10-gallon can and continued to soak the vines and ground. It had been a warm late spring and Bobby Pierce had been forced to irrigate the vines recently. The figure wanted to be sure the fire would catch.

He could smell the gasoline. The fumes made his eyes water. He stepped back onto the road and grabbed the newspapers he'd carried down to the field with him. He rolled several sheets to create a wick and soaked one end with the last of his gasoline.

He snapped his lighter and lit the end. A whoosh of flame caught him off guard, but he quickly threw the newspaper into the vines. They quickly caught and began to burn. He could hear it snap and crackle.

He wished he'd brought more gasoline, but it had been heavy. He lit a few more rolls of newspaper and started fires further in the rows. He was careful to keep from getting too close to the fires, which were beginning to grow.

He quickly gathered the empty gas cans and hurried back toward the winery buildings. He needed to hide the gas cans inside the shed. He was sweating by the time he got back to the winery and his heart raced.

He'd done it! And he looked forward to the money he was expecting to be paid for tonight's work.

Laura and Bobby were awakened in the pre-dawn hours to shouts from the workers from the fields. Someone banged on Bobby's front door.

"Fire! Fire! Bobby, there's fire in the vines!"

Bobby sat bolt up, reaching for his pants and a shirt. "Stay here!" he said.

Bobby rushed out of the house to more shouts and yelling.

Laura was concerned. Fire? Where? In the winery? Oh God, she thought, this will be bad publicity. She quickly got dressed, pulled on a jacket and walked out of the house to find Bobby.

She could smell the acrid scent of smoke in the air. It definitely wasn't the woodsy smell of last night's fireplace fire.

Laura, with her low-heeled boots on, ran toward the thick black smoke she could see at the far end of the winery. Her blisters on her feet burned as she ran. She could see the reddish hue as she drew closer to the far end of the winery.

Men were running everywhere. The winery was chaotic. She could hear sirens in the distance, thankfully getting closer.

Laura could see the red Napa County fire engines coming along the far side of the winery, along a road on the side.

Firemen quickly pulled hoses out and began dousing the fire. Laura was in awe of the efficiency of the firemen and prayed the tanker truck held enough water to put out the fire.

The water spray arced over the far vines. She could see someone had also turned on the irrigation system, trying to help put out the fire. The irrigation system began spraying the vines, then sputtered and went out.

As the fire got under control, the smoke turned more gray than black, then whiter than gray. She recognized many of the winery hands milling about, but she didn't know their names. They seemed to know her. They nodded their heads at her as they passed. A couple of them tipped their cowboy hats. Even in a crisis, they had grabbed their cowboy hats, she mused.

Laura smiled and nodded in the early dawn light. She stood there a little while longer, pulling her jacket around her.

The colors at dawn were so beautiful in contrast to the red, white and blue flashing lights of the emergency vehicles. Law enforcement vehicles had shown up as well and the blue strobe lights hurt her eyes.

She turned and began to walk back to Bobby's house. She couldn't be of any help until later, when crisis communication for the winery would be necessary. She needed to craft a statement for the press she knew would be calling.

When Laura got back to Bobby's house, she could hear her cellphone ringing and saw she'd missed five calls and had three voicemails. This was going to be a long day, she thought.

But first things first. She stripped down and got in Bobby's shower, warming her muscles that had gone cold in the chilly morning air. As she toweled off, she heard the front door open and Bobby call out, "Laura!"

"I'm in the bathroom. I just got out of the shower," she called out through the bathroom door.

Bobby poked his head into the steamy air of the bathroom. "I need your help. News media are all over the place."

"I'm on it. Let me do all the talking. Don't say anything to them. Don't make any statement. I'll do all of that for you."

Bobby looked relieved. "OK. I was hoping you would. I don't like talking to the press."

Laura was sorry she hadn't packed a more professional suit for the trip to Napa. She didn't think she would need one. And she didn't have time to go to a boutique shop to buy one.

She put on a pair of jeans, the deep green long-sleeved cotton blouse and her cowboy boots. Her feet still rebelled at her blisters, which had reopened. She'd put on a couple more bandages, but she'd just have to take more ibuprofen and deal with the pain. She tried to tie her hair into a messy bun, but it was still wet.

"Where are the media?" she asked Bobby.

"Down by the fire, getting photos."

"OK. I'll head that way."

"I can take you down in the ATV."

"Oh my God. My feet will thank you."

Bobby smiled and kissed Laura. "Told you so," he whispered.

Laura shoved him playfully in the chest. "Don't you even start."

"Come on. I really don't want those reporters tramping through my vines."

"How bad is it?" Laura asked.

"I can't really tell."

"How did it start?"

"No idea. The fire department investigators and the fire marshal are out there now."

"OK. Let's go."

Chapter 15

Laura felt a thrill as she stood before television cameras and microphones and answered questions as best she could about the fire at Star 1. She and the reporters stood away from the fire scene, where fire investigators were milling about with cameras and dogs.

This was what she was meant to do. She felt it in her blood.

"What caused the fire?" one reporter asked.

"The fire marshal's investigators are working to figure out how the fire started. You will have to direct your questions to him," she answered.

"Do you think this was an accident or arson?" another asked.

"It is very premature to know what the cause of the fire is. The fire marshal and his team are on the scene now. I'm sure they will be thorough in their investigation."

"How long will the investigation take?" a third asked.

"The fire marshal has told me he expects the investigation to take several days. I will give each of you my email address. Please email me your contact information and I will send out an update at 4 p.m. each day, in time for your evening news," Laura said, handing out a quickly printed press release with her email address on it. She hesitated to give out her cell number, for fear she'd get calls at all hours. She knew how reporters were. They could be like dogs that won't give up a bone in her opinion.

Laura certainly felt like she was earning her keep now. She'd have to call Kyle as soon as this impromptu press conference was over to let him know about the fire and how she was handling it. Maybe he'd put her on a retainer. She'd certainly suggest it when she talked to him.

When the press conference ended, reporters and photographers went closer to the fire scene, hoping to get photos and interview the fire marshal. Laura trailed behind them. She didn't want to be surprised if the fire marshal said anything bad about the fire or winery.

Laura needn't have worried. He had less to say than she did, telling the reporters he'd have no comment until his report was complete, and that could take several days.

Laura spotted Bobby talking to one of the fire investigators. He did not look happy.

He looked up and saw her, nodding his head toward her. Laura turned and started back toward the office. She'd make a call to Kyle to update him and request he put her on a retainer for the time being. Her work from her on out was not going to be free.

Laura's call went to voicemail. "Mr. Quitman, this is Laura Lucas. There has been a fire at the winery. The fire marshal is here investigating. I've handled the media that arrived this morning, but I'm asking you to put me on a retainer until the investigation is over, which should be in a few days. Please call me back at your convenience."

Laura hung up just as Bobby entered the office.

"I just left a message for Quitman about the fire," she said.

Bobby's face darkened. "I wish you had talked to me before you called him," he barked. "I am the guy in charge."

"I know you are in charge. Why did I need to discuss it with you first? He has a right to know about the fire at his property."

"I know he has a right to know about it," Bobby said, his voice tight. "The fire marshal thinks it may be arson. That's why the dogs were there, to see if they smelled accelerants."

"Arson? Oh shit. Who would do that to the winery? To you? Are there some enemies of yours you haven't told me about?"

"I don't have any enemies that I know of. I sure have folks that want to see me fail, but I can't believe they'd set fire to my property."

"Well friends don't set fires at your business."

"No, they don't." Bobby paced back and forth in the small office. "One of the fire marshal's investigators is asking where I was last night. I told him I was with you. You are my alibi."

"Why would you need an alibi? Does he suspect you?"

"Her. It's a woman. And I don't know if I'm a suspect. I was in debt with the winery. That's no secret. But I sold a majority share to Quitman."

"I was with you last night and unless you can time travel you were beside me all night," Laura said. "I'll tell her you were with me."

Laura's cellphone rang. It was Kyle Quitman.

"Hello, Mr. Quitman. Bobby is here with me. Let me put you on speaker."

"What's this about a fire?" Kyle asked. "How bad is it?"

"It looks like it's about 30 acres," Bobby said. "It was contained fairly quickly on the far side of the winery."

"How did it start?" Kyle asked.

"The fire marshal investigator thinks it may be arson, sir."

"Arson? Who the hell would want to burn me out?"

Bobby rankled at Kyle's word "me." It was Bobby's winery, even if he didn't own it anymore. "I can't tell you that, sir. I can give the investigator your number. I'm sure she'll want to talk to you, too," Bobby answered.

"Laura, what have you been doing to contain the news?" Kyle asked.

"Well, I held a press conference for the media that showed up here this morning. I didn't give them any information about the arson because I just learned that myself. I've given them my point of contact for any more information and I told them I'd be releasing updates at four o'clock each afternoon, so they can get it on the evening news."

"I don't want too much publicity about this, Laura," Kyle said.

"There is no such thing as too much publicity, sir. This gets Star 1's name out there, even if this is not such good news. We also have a nice feature about to come out in a couple of weeks in one of the lifestyle magazines, featuring the event space at the winery. As soon as we can get access to the website, I'll update that too. And my next update will say there is no change to the operations here. It's business as usual."

Laura looked at Bobby and mouthed 'It is business as usual? Yes?'

Bobby nodded.

"Laura, I will put you on a retainer for a week. I can extend it if needed, but you have to send me reasons why it would need to be extended. Send me your proposal, and make sure you give me each update before you send them to the reporters."

"Of course."

Kyle hung up without saying goodbye.

"Nice guy," Bobby said.

"I'm sure he's busy," Laura said, trying to defend Kyle. She'd worked with CEOs and she knew they could often be abrupt on the phone.

"Busy making millions."

"Don't take it so personally. Why do you dislike him so much? Especially if you sold most of your winery to him?"

"That guy was born with a silver spoon in his mouth. He probably has never had to work a hard day in his life. Have you ever shaken his hands? They are smooth as a baby's bottom. Not a callus or cut on them."

Bobby held out his own scarred and callused hands in front of Laura. Laura took Bobby's hands in hers.

"I love your hands. I love your rough skin when it touches mine. But my hands are just as smooth as his."

"I sure as hell don't want Kyle's hands touching me the way you do," he grinned.

"I should hope not," she smiled back. "I have a proposal to send Kyle, so I'd better get to work."

"And I need to get back into the vines. I need to find out why the irrigation system didn't work right during the fire. I had my foreman turn it on and it quit almost immediately."

Laura's eyebrows wrinkled. "The irrigation system didn't work? The one that shot water out at us the other day?"

"Yes. I need to check it. I think it might have been tampered with," Bobby frowned, then brightened. "Will I see you later tonight?"

"I need to go back to the hotel at some point to shower and get another change of clothes. And I need to do laundry."

"Bring your clothes here. Do your wash at my house. I'll see you later then."

Laura returned to her hotel shortly after lunch. She'd grabbed a sandwich on the way back and quickly ate it in her room before she showered.

She packed a clean set of clothes and threw her dirty clothes in the hotel's laundry bag. She was relieved she could wash her clothes at Bobby's house. That would save her a little money. She felt like she was bleeding money, but he was glad she was now on retainer.

Then she called the fire marshal's office to see if she could get an update from the investigator. She'd learned the name of the investigator was Sgt. Rebecca Gladwell.

Laura had to leave a message for Sgt. Gladwell. If she didn't get an update from the investigator, she would write an update for the media with a "nothing new to report" statement and send it to Kyle before she sent it to the press.

Laura had sent the retainer proposal to Kyle earlier in the day. She'd asked for $10,000, but expected he'd counter for half of that. Much to her surprise, he sent back his signature on the proposal for the full amount.

Laura almost wept with relief. She'd be able to make her mortgage payment for July. Then she frowned. Maybe she should have asked for more. Ten thousand dollars was probably Quitman's dry-cleaning bill, she thought.

Laura pulled into the winery and noticed Bobby's truck was gone. She didn't have a key to the office or to his house, so she sat in her rental car for a while, typing out emails on her laptop.

After 20 minutes, she texted Bobby. **I'm at the winery, where are you?**

She got no response. Laura tossed her cellphone in the passenger's seat and returned to her laptop. She was grateful she could pick up the office's Wi-Fi from her car if she parked close enough to the door.

Another 20 minutes passed. Now Laura began to get irritated. She didn't know where Bobby was, she was locked out of the office and he wasn't responding to her texts or calls. She was bored and starting to get looks from the workers at the winery.

Laura grabbed her jacket and got out of her car, deciding to walk down to the burned area of the winery.

When she got to the burned area, she could still smell the acrid scent of the fire. If she inhaled, she could taste it on her tongue.

Laura came up to the yellow crime tape and ducked under it. The ground was muddy from all the water of the fire hoses. She tried to miss the deep puddles and mud as best she could. She didn't want to ruin her nice boots.

She walked around what was now a crime scene. She didn't see anything that caught her attention. Why should it? She didn't know what she was looking for. After all, the investigators had been here before her. Surely, they had seen everything there was to see.

Laura walked further along the burnt-out vine rows when she saw what looked like a deflated balloon in the charred vines. What was that? She wondered. She reached out and grabbed it.

She looked at it, turning it over in her hands. It was white and plastic. Should she bring it back to the office? Should she tell the fire investigator about it? Well, she knew Sgt. Gladwell had been out here to the scene. Surely, she had seen this and dismissed it.

Laura tossed the white plastic balloon back in the charred vines where she found it. She couldn't imagine it was anything of value to the investigation.

She began her trek back to the winery's office. She was hoping Bobby would be back there. She checked her iPhone but didn't see a message from him. She expected she'd get back to the office and not see him there. Laura knew she'd be returning to her hotel soon.

Laura got back to the office, checked the locked door and turned to her rental car. She got in and began her drive down the winery and turned right toward her hotel. She was hoping she'd hear from Bobby. She wanted to feel him on top of her tonight.

About nine o'clock that night Laura got a call from Bobby.

"Where have you been?" she demanded, answering curtly.

"Well hello to you too, darling," he responded.

"I waited a long time at the office and you weren't there. Where were you?"

"I was down at the police station being grilled by Sgt. Gladwell and detective Morris about the arson."

"Why?"

"Someone in this town is spreading rumors that I set the fire."

"Did you set the fire, Bobby?" Laura asked, concerned.

"I can't believe you'd even ask me that. I'd never do that to my own place."

"It's not your place anymore," Laura said flatly. "Maybe you set it for revenge on Kyle, or is there an insurance policy on the place?"

"No insurance on this place in my name anymore. I signed that all over to Kyle," Bobby said, angry. "And what about you? You could have set the fire."

"Me? Why would I do that? And what the fuck? I have no vested interest in the winery," Laura shot back.

"You don't? Wouldn't you make more money if you had to do damage control because of the fire? I bet you did set it," Bobby spat.

"You are out of your fucking mind, Bobby. I did not set the fire. I was asleep right next to you that night, you bastard. But maybe you did, or you had that friend of yours do a 'favor' for you."

"What the hell does that mean?" Bobby shouted into the phone.

"It means you didn't want me in that meeting in San Francisco. Didn't want me to hear whatever favor you were asking your friend to do."

"You are one crazy bitch with a wild imagination. Favors? I offered him several cases of our wine at a discount so he'd push the wine to the restaurants he distributes to."

"Well why couldn't I be in that meeting then? What was the big secret?"

"I don't want to discuss my fucking business in front of you. It's my fucking business, not yours."

"Bobby Pierce, you are 100 percent an asshole," Laura said, hanging up on him.

Laura was mad. And now she wasn't going to get laid tonight. She was really regretting she hadn't packed her vibrator on this trip.

Laura had paced her hotel after having a late dinner. Before she could think better of it, Laura dialed Lee Adams' cell number.

"Hello?" said a sleepy male voice on the other end.

"Oh, Lee? This is Laura. I'm sorry to call so late. I'm sorry to wake you. I'll call back tomorrow."

"No, it's alright," he said. "What do you need?"

Laura hesitated. What she needed was a good screw. But now that she had called Lee, she wasn't so sure she should have called him.

Furious with Bobby, she'd called Lee on impulse. She knew he desired her.

"Well, I didn't mean to disturb you. I just wondered if you wanted a late-night drink — at your house."

Lee Adams was quiet for a moment. "At my house?"

"Well, you could come to my hotel. I have some Star 1 wine in the room, but that buttery Chardonnay you had the other night was delightful."

"Oh, you'd like to come here?"

"I would, if that's OK."

"That's OK. Are you coming here now?"

Laura could hear the click of a light, probably a bedside lamp.

"As soon as I can get down to my car."

"Well, then, I'll see you soon."

Laura pulled up to Lee's house and hesitated. In the back of her mind, she knew sleeping with Lee was a bad idea. But when had Laura ever thought twice about a bad idea? Laura felt like her old self, taking control of men and her life.

Lee opened his front door as Laura opened her car door.

Two glasses of the Chardonnay were on the small table by the couch.

"Tonight is such a lovely evening," Lee said. "I have a heavy sweater if you'd like to sit outside on the patio."

"Sure," Laura said, accepting the thick sweater he held for her as she slipped her arms through. "This is nice and warm."

"You'll need it. It is nippy, but you can see the stars really well tonight."

Lee moved over to some patio chaises and Laura sat in one of them, careful not to spill her wine. He pulled the other chaise over to be near her.

After he settled in his chaise, he asked, "What made you change your mind?"

"Change my mind about what?"

"Coming over to spend the night with me."

"What makes you think I'm spending the night with you?" Laura asked. "All I'm doing is having a nightcap with you."

"We both know you are lying, Laura."

Laura smiled in the darkness. "The stars are very bright tonight. I never get to see stars like this in Atlanta. Too much light pollution."

"You are changing the subject."

"What if I am? A woman can change her mind."

"Very well. I'm just glad you did change your mind. I thought you and Bobby Pierce were an item. And you know the word is he set the fire at his place."

Laura very nearly blurted that Bobby couldn't have started the fire because he was in bed with her that night. She took a breath to speak, then closed her mouth.

"I hadn't heard that," she said instead.

"I'd be careful of him if I were you. I think I told you he's got a bit of a reputation in this town."

"I'll keep that in mind. But can we not talk about Bobby Pierce right now? I just want to enjoy the wine and the evening."

"Of course."

The pair fell silent. Laura sipped at her Chardonnay and Lee stood up to retrieve the bottle.

"May I top you off?" he asked.

Laura held up her half empty glass and Lee poured more of the golden liquid in it. Then he poured more into his glass.

Lee settled back in his chaise, pulling a blanket over his legs. "What do you want to talk about?"

"Tell me how you got into photography."

"A lot of that is on my website, in my bio," he replied.

"That is all pretty dry. What made you take up the profession of photography?"

"I was in the audio/visual department in high school. I was one of those nerdy guys who never got the girls. But I did learn how to develop film. And it was film for me back in the day, with the chemicals and the dark room."

"Lee you aren't THAT old," Laura chided.

"Our high school wasn't that fancy. Other schools had digital cameras at their disposal, we did not. My high school was on the lower socio-economic scale. We had old Nikon and Canon 35mm cameras that our photography teacher would find in pawn shops. He'd get them working and we learned on those cameras."

"It sounds like you enjoyed your time in high school," she remarked.

"I hated it," Lee said, with some bitterness. "If it weren't for the photography class and the photography teacher, I probably would have dropped out and joined the military. I wasn't very good in school. My grades weren't that great. And I wasn't all that cool with the girls, until they needed me to shoot their prom photos or the homecoming court. I'd be out at the prom shooting candids or at the football games shooting the cheerleaders or the homecoming king and queen. I made them look good. No, I made them look great."

"Did you get the girls then?"

Lee laughed. "No. They were more than willing to use me for my skills, but not my chubby teen-aged body. I graduated from high school a virgin."

Laura was quiet. She would have graduated from high school a virgin, too, if she hadn't gotten involved with Julio. She shuddered at the thought.

"Are you cold? Maybe we should go inside," Lee said, noticing Laura's shudder.

"Yes, let's go inside."

Lee collected the empty wine bottle and folded his blanket over the chaise. He then ushered Laura back into his warm home.

"Shall I open another bottle?"

"I'm fine for tonight, thank you. But if you want another glass go right ahead."

"I think I'm done for the night, too."

Lee put the empty wine bottle in his recycle bin and then reached for Laura's wine glass, giving hers and his a rinse in the sink before placing them on the counter. "I'll wash those up later."

Lee turned to face Laura, taking her hands in his. Laura could feel his smooth hands. Not hands that worked at a winery.

Lee's hands cupped her face and he kissed her gently, then with more passion. His hands slid under her shirt, slipping them under her bra. His cool hands felt so soft and smooth as he caressed her breasts and nipples, which got erect at his touch.

Laura closed her eyes. She didn't want to think about Bobby tonight. Not tonight.

Chapter 16

Laura awoke next to Lee, who had his hand on her hip. For someone who had been a virgin when he graduated high school, Lee certainly had learned his way around a female body.

Sunlight peeked through the light-yellow curtains of the bedroom, giving the room a soft golden glow.

Laura stretched, raising her arms and pointing her toes. She felt Lee stir next to her.

"Good morning," he said, his dirty blond hair falling into his eyes. He pushed back his hair and rubbed the blond stubble on his chin.

"Good morning. Did you sleep well?"

"I slept great. Nothing like a good night of sex to put me in a sound slumber."

"Glad I could be of service," Laura said, rolling over toward him.

"I didn't mean it that way. I just meant…"

"I know what you meant. I didn't take offense," Laura said, sitting up and looking around for her clothes. "I guess I better get back to my hotel."

Lee reached for her arm. "You sure? We could make love again. And I've got some really good weed."

Laura smiled. "I think I'd better go."

"Will I see you again tonight?" Lee asked hopefully.

"We'll see."

Lee frowned. "I know what that means."

"What does that mean?"

"It means I won't see you tonight," he said, frowning. "It means I was just your good-time boy last night."

"You certainly were a good time, Lee," Laura said, trying to give him her easy smile. "Don't take this the wrong way, but sometimes a woman has an itch that needs to be scratched, too. Last night, Lee, I had an itch. You certainly scratched it."

"Glad I could be of service," he said bitterly.

"Don't be that way. It was a good time for you, too. Let's not leave angry."

Laura, dressed now, grabbed her purse and her keys and headed for the front door. "Goodbye, Lee. I'll see you soon."

Laura closed the door behind her and headed for her car. She could see Lee glaring at her through his front window. He looked angry. Laura was now regretting her bad idea.

She looked at her cellphone and saw several missed calls from Bobby, then a text: **Where are you? I'm at your hotel and your car isn't here.**

Oh shit, Laura thought. She never expected he'd go to her hotel to look for her. She'd have to come up with some lie to tell Bobby. She certainly didn't want to say she'd spent the night with Lee.

Laura pulled into the parking lot of her hotel and quickly scanned the trucks in the parking lot to make sure Bobby wasn't waiting for her. He wasn't. Laura felt a wave of relief.

She got to her room, showered and just made it to the free breakfast with ten minutes to spare. It was lukewarm scrambled eggs, lukewarm bacon and fresh toast. But the coffee was still hot. Again, she dumped lots of sugar in it.

When Laura got back to her room, she texted Bobby with the excuse she's gone for a drive the night before and gotten lost, returning to the hotel very late. She hoped he'd believe it. Laura had gone for a drive last night alright, but it was straight to Lee's house.

Laura decided she'd work at a nearby coffee house that day, avoiding both Bobby and Lee.

She checked in with Sgt. Gladwell at the fire department, learning the arson case was still active. Laura realized she'd only learn about the case when an arrest was likely. She hoped Bobby was not involved. She honestly couldn't be sure.

Laura knew he had been with her the night before, but what if that was just so he could have an alibi? She still doubted his excuse about the business meeting in San Francisco. But why would he set fire to a winery he clearly loved? That part didn't make senses to her.

Who else might start the fire? A rival vintner? A fire bug? Laura expected Sgt. Gladwell might question her as well. It made her nervous. She didn't have anything to hide, she realized, but she didn't want to become an item in the news, either.

By early afternoon, Laura got another cup of coffee and a small sandwich, but she was tired of working at the coffee house.

She finished her small lunch and returned to her hotel. The four walls of her room seemed so small and to close in on her. She was tired of California. This job was more than she'd bargained for.

Laura paced her room trying to figure out her next move. She needed to give a report to Kyle Quitman before she sent a press release to the news media, although she could sense the story was waning. There were other stories, sexier stories, to chase.

At this rate, Quitman wasn't going to continue her retainer. Laura would certainly like to work for $10,000 for another week. That was a hefty retainer. But she realized the chance of that happening was slim; not unless something big broke open on the arson story.

Laura didn't even want to think of what might cause the arson story to break open. She shuddered when she thought of the possibilities: Bobby being arrested for the arson or being arrested for hiring someone to start the fire. Could he really do that? Could he really do that to a winery that appeared to be his passion?

Laura had her doubts that he could do that, but she also had her doubts that his hands were entirely clean. When it came down to it, Laura enjoyed him for his lovemaking, but really didn't trust him. And a man she couldn't trust was always a man to be wary of.

She'd trusted a man before and look where that had gotten her. Assaulted and pregnant. She shook her head to clear the bad memories.

Laura jumped when her cellphone rang. It was Bobby.

"Hello, Bobby," she said, her voice calm and smooth.

"Where were you last night?" he demanded.

"I told you. I went for a drive last night and got lost. I got back to the hotel very late."

"How late?"

"Why do you want to know, Bobby? Were you at my hotel spying on me?"

"I was at your hotel until 2 a.m. Did you get lost for that long?"

"Well, I must have just missed you then."

"You were with Lee, weren't you?"

"Bobby, what is going on with you? Why are you acting this way? Did something happen with the police?"

"You are changing the subject, Laura."

"Because I'm genuinely concerned for you. You seem very paranoid. Is everything OK with you?"

"Will you come over tonight?"

"Do you want me to? You seemed very angry when we left last night," Laura said, hesitant to go to see Bobby.

"You were the one who flipped me off," he said with sarcasm.

"You completely pissed me off," she said, her voice rising.

"Well, will you come over tonight?"

"Do you want my company, or do you just want to screw?"

"I want both."

"Well, you are honest."

"I find honesty is the best policy."

"Do you? Do you really?"

"What do you mean by THAT?" Bobby demanded.

"Did you set that fire, Bobby, or pay someone to do it for you?"

"Listen, Laura, we've been over that," he said, his voice tight. "I'm tired of people whispering rumors that I set the fire and I'm tired of being accused of something I didn't do!"

At the end of his sentence, Bobby was shouting into the phone.

"OK, OK. Calm down, Bobby. I'll come over now. I just want you to keep that temper under control."

"I can keep it under control unless I'm being accused of something I didn't do!" Bobby hung up, not giving Laura a chance to reply.

He is such an asshole, Laura thought, looking at her cellphone. But he's an asshole who fucks so well.

Laura arrived at the winery in the early evening. She pulled up next to Bobby's pickup truck in front of his house. She didn't knock at the front door, just opened it and walked in.

She found Bobby pacing the floor in the living room.

"Why are you so antsy?" She asked.

"I feel like I'm going to come out of my skin. The reporters have started calling me asking for a comment on the rumors."

"They have? Do not talk to them!" Laura insisted. "Come on, let's go for a walk."

"A walk?"

"It will do us both good to get out and walk the vineyard. It will be good for you to get out into your element," Laura said, putting her hand on Bobby's chest, rubbing her hand in a small circle.

"OK. I could use a walk outside."

They stepped outside and Bobby took Laura's hand. She looked down at his fingers entwined in hers but didn't pull away.

They walked down the path toward the site of the arson.

"Did you mean to come here?" Bobby asked.

"Not really. I was down here the other day and I found something, but I'm sure the investigators didn't miss it."

"What was it?" Bobby asked, excited.

"It looked like an old balloon. It was over there among the rocks," Laura said, pointing to the edge of the vineyard.

"Where?"

"I don't know where. I found it, picked it up and put it back."

"That might have been evidence!" Bobby shouted. "Why didn't you take it to the fire investigator?"

"I just figured they'd been over this whole place. I didn't think it was anything."

"Maybe it was something. Help me look for what you saw," he said, beginning to frantically look in the burned edges of the vines. "Where was it?"

"I told you I don't know. I don't remember."

Bobby whirled around and grabbed Laura by the arms. "Try to remember!" he said, shaking her.

"Get your hands off of me!" Laura said through gritted teeth. She shook his hands off her and began walking quickly back to the path and back to the house.

"Where are you going?" he yelled toward her back. "Help me look!" She turned to face Bobby. "I'm going back to my hotel."

Bobby jogged up beside her, grabbing her by the arm. "No, please. Please. Please help me look. It could be something. It could be something that stops the rumors. Please help me," he said softly.

Laura stopped and turned back as Bobby led her back to where they'd come. Bobby took Laura's hand again and began pulling her toward the burned edges of the vines.

"What did you say it looked like?" he asked.

"It looked like a deflated balloon. Like a white balloon."

They searched the right side of the path, where Laura said she had found it, in more of the rocky area, not the burned edges of the vines. They'd walked for at least a quarter mile when Laura pointed to a white object. "I think that's it."

"This?" he asked, holding up what really did look like an old balloon. Bobby frowned. "I think this is from the party we had when you and Marc Linder were here."

"Then why isn't it burned up? Everything here is burned."

"I don't know," he said, turning the piece of plastic over in his hand. He then put it in his front pocket. "I'll bring it to Sgt. Gladwell. I just hope she doesn't laugh me out of Napa County."

They walked back to the house, hand in hand. Bobby seemed calmer now and Laura felt the tension easing from her shoulders. Bobby dropped Laura's hand and wrapped his arm around her shoulder, pulling her close.

"Want to go inside and forget about the arson?"

"You have a great way of persuasion."

"Persuasion. I have a great way with my dick in your pussy. And you like it," Bobby said.

"Bobby, you have such a way with words," Laura smiled a little wicked smile. "And yes, Bobby, yes I do like your dick in my pussy."

Bobby pulled Laura into the house and straight into his bedroom.

Once again, Laura heard Bobby's alarm go off in the darkness of the pre-dawn morning.

Laura roused herself in Bobby's bedroom, realizing she was not in her hotel room. She was beginning to think she shouldn't have rented the hotel, just asked Bobby if she could stay at his place.

Then she remembered her night with Lee. She'd spent the night with Lee because she was pissed off at Bobby. She'd never be able to live with Bobby, however short a stay it might be. They'd be at each other's throats in no time.

Bobby rolled over out of the bed. "I've got chores to do this morning."

"It's just slam, bam, thank you ma'am?" Laura mocked.

"Hey, I hear there's a great breakfast at your hotel," Bobby said snidely. "I think you should go eat it."

Laura got up, grabbing her clothes off the floor. "You are a real asshole, Bobby!" she shouted.

"You've told me more than once."

Laura left Bobby's house angry again. Why was he such a bastard after they had a great night of sex? she wondered. He must have started the fire, she thought as she got in her rental car and pulled out of the winery's driveway.

When she arrived at her hotel she got to her room, showered and headed down to breakfast. Today's breakfast was a cheese omelet, breakfast sausage, toast. She put some butter and strawberry jam on her toast.

She was beginning to think she should have oatmeal, yogurt and fruit, just for a healthier breakfast, but she tucked into the omelet, sausage and toast.

Laura realized when she got back to Atlanta, she'd have to hit the gym and drop about five pounds, maybe more. Her clothes were starting to feel a little tight.

She'd be ready for a Pilates class and a massage when she got back.

Laura returned to her room, emailed the reporters asking when the stories about Star 1 would run, emailed Lee asking if the video and photos were ready to put on the website, if his guy had gotten the password to the website, and finally Kyle, saying she needed another week of retainer to keep her role as crisis manager for Star 1 winery.

She hadn't been "crisis manager" for a whole week yet, and she wasn't quite sure Kyle would give her a role as a temporary "crisis manager" for a little while longer, but it couldn't hurt to ask. Besides, she could definitely use another $10,000 for a second week.

Not bad work before 11 a.m., she thought to herself.

Once again Laura was antsy. She went online to look for a good place to have lunch. She really would have to hit the gym when she got back home.

What else was there to do out here in Napa Valley? Eat, sleep, drink good wine and have sex. Oh, and meet with reporters when necessary and try to convince them to write nice stories about Star 1.

Laura threw her cellphone onto the bed, still mad since she'd spent the previous night with Bobby. Once again, she found herself pacing her small hotel room.

She went to the window and pulled the curtain to let in more light. The sky was bright blue, but she knew it was cool outside.

Laura jumped when her cellphone rang. She saw Bobby's name and answered it.

"Are you done with your chores?" she snapped.

"Well, hello to you, too, Laura. As a matter of fact, I am done with this morning's chores. I'm ready for lunch. Will you pick up a sandwich for me and bring it out to the winery?"

Laura's face and voice grew tight. "Am I just a delivery service now?"

"Of course not, bring one for yourself, too. We'll have a working lunch. Discuss what we need to do next. It will be a business expense, right?"

Laura sighed deeply. "Where do you want me to go for your sandwich?"

"Just go to Subway. It's quick and easy."

"Subway?" Laura asked in disbelief.

"Yeah. I like Subway. Get me a turkey sandwich, all the fixings. And chips and a Coke."

"Anything else, sir?" Laura asked with sarcasm.

"And a chocolate chip cookie. Please."

"Your wish is my command," Laura said, and hung up.

Laura drove up the driveway to the winery and pulled up in front of Bobby's house. She got out, saw him standing outside the front door, and threw his Subway sandwich bag at him. Caught off guard, Bobby juggled the bag, nearly dropping it. He half expected Laura would throw his soft drink at him, too.

"Hey!" he said. "Don't be mad."

"I am mad. I'm not your serving wench," Laura said, shouting at Bobby in front of his house. Winery hands nearby turned to look at the pair.

One worker watched them with interest. He reached into his pocket and felt the large wad of cash there. This would pay off his gambling debts, he thought. His wife would never find out about it.

Bobby saw they were being watched and pulled Laura by the arm into the house. "I never said you were! Why are you always busting my balls, Laura?"

"I'm not busting your balls. I may be sucking them, but not busting them."

"Yes, you are. I just wanted to have lunch with you, and you are making a federal issue out of it."

Laura walked back out of the door and to her car. Bobby thought she might be leaving, but instead she reached in the passenger seat and got her own Subway sandwich bag. She also brought out a cardboard box that held two soft drinks, balancing it in her hands, the plastic sandwich bag swinging free in her left hand.

Bobby held the door for her and she walked back in the house and placed the drinks down on the kitchen counter and her sandwich bag. Bobby reached into the upper kitchen cabinets and grabbed two white plates.

He placed them on the small kitchenette table, then pulled out a kitchen chair for Laura. Laura raised her eyebrows in surprise.

"I can be a gentleman," Bobby said.

"Nice to know," Laura said, sitting down. Bobby pushed her chair in for her.

Bobby sat down, pulling his sandwich out of his bag, as well as a bag of chips. Laura did the same.

Bobby ate voraciously, gulping his sandwich down in big mouthfuls. Laura ate more daintily, eating slowly. Bobby finished his lunch in just minutes, while Laura wasn't even halfway through her meal.

Bobby sat back in his chair, burping. He didn't even try to cover it up, Laura thought, her mouth tightening.

Bobby caught the look on her face and quickly said, "Excuse me, Laura. Good sandwich. Thank you."

Laura gave a tight smile. "You're welcome. Anything else I can do for you today?"

"Well, I have a couple of hours before my next set of chores."

Now Laura eased her smile. "Oh really? Anything you have in mind to pass those hours?"

"Well, I could polish my boots."

"Your boots? Is that all you want to polish?"

"I usually use wax to make my boots shine. I could take out my wax."

"And wax just your boots?"

"What would you like me to wax besides my boots?"

"I'd like you to wax my pussy," Laura said, putting her sandwich down, half eaten, and looking Bobby straight in his eyes.

"Really, now? I'd say your pussy is already well waxed. But maybe there's something else I can do for you. Let's move into the bedroom and see what happens."

"Have you ever made love outside?" Laura asked.

Bobby raised an eyebrow. "Outside? In daylight?"

"Grab a blanket and let's go down to the far side of the vineyard, where it's a little more remote."

A figure stepped out of the shadows near the house and watched Laura and Bobby walk down the path into the vineyard. He thought about following them but turned and went back to the shed.

Chapter 17

Bobby and Laura walked back up to the house holding hands. Bobbly leaned over to kiss Laura on the side of her head. Then he brushed some leaves out of her hair. Laura quickly tried to finger brush her thick black hair, but she knew it was probably messy from the intense lovemaking they'd just had.

Outside in the open, Bobby had almost been like an animal, his primal instinct taking over. Laura felt herself reaching climax not once but twice. She nearly cried out, but Bobby put his hand over her mouth. Winery workers would have heard what they were doing, even though they'd found a remote spot on a far corner in the vines.

When it was over, Laura's nerves were on end, vibrating with excitement. She loved having sex outside. She loved the adrenaline rush it gave her.

Laura looked over at Bobby to gauge his reaction as they lay on the blanket. She couldn't quite read the expression in his eyes, which were half closed. His breathing was getting more even now. But she had a feeling he'd enjoyed it too.

They'd remained naked for a while after they'd made love, Bobby pulling part of the blanket over both of them.

Laura curled up next to Bobby, enjoying the warmth of his body and the heat of their spent lovemaking. Eventually, she told Bobby she was cold, and they gathered their clothes and got dressed, then headed up to the house.

Laura was surprised that even in the late afternoon in Napa it could be quite cool. In Atlanta, when she'd made love outside in June, she'd ended up sweaty and gross, but nevertheless satisfied. This afternoon she wasn't sweaty and still very satisfied.

When they returned to the house, Laura asked, "Can you start a fire? I'm still chilly."

"Let me get you the comforter," Bobby said, going into his bedroom and returning with the multicolored quilt Laura once wrapped herself in just weeks ago.

He placed it on her shoulders and she wrapped the rest of the quilt around her body. Laura shivered.

"Can I make you a cup of coffee or tea? That will warm you up."

Laura nodded and shivered again. "I guess I caught a chill outside."

"I hope you're not coming down with something."

"I hope not, too. The last thing I want to be is sick while I'm out here. I won't be able to do my job. Do you have any vitamin C or echinacea?"

"Echinacea? What do you need that crap for?" Bobby asked, reaching up into a kitchen cabinet and pulling down a bottle of bourbon. "Here, drink this," he said, pouring out a small portion in a low-ball glass and handing it to Laura. He filled another glass for himself.

Laura took the glass and turned it in her hand, watching the amber liquid begin to swirl as she circled her hand. "Is this a decent bottle?"

"Of course. I only have the best wine and I only have the best bourbon."

Laura put the glass to her lips and swallowed the bourbon in one gulp. Her eyes began to water and she tried not to choke.

"Jesus, Laura, sip it. That bourbon is $150 a bottle. It's too expensive to drink like that."

Laura coughed then held out her glass for a refill. Bobby looked at her with skepticism but poured a lesser amount of bourbon in her glass. Laura kept holding her glass to him and he filled it with more.

"Sip it this time," he insisted. Then Bobby raised his glass to his lips, took a small sip, swirling it around in his mouth, letting the taste wash over his tongue before he swallowed. "That is damn good bourbon."

Laura smiled, raised her glass and sipped her drink this time, following his lead, letting the amber liquid roll over her tongue.

"This does taste good."

"Told you to sip it. Are you getting warm?"

"Yes. Yes, I am," Laura said, giving Bobby a little smile.

"Laura, is everything sex with you?"

"Not everything," she said defensively. She smiled wider. "But when it comes to you, well maybe."

Bobby walked over to face Laura. "Why with me?"

"Why not with you?"

"No, Laura. Tell me why you think that way with me."

Laura took Bobby's hand, turning it over and rubbing the palm of her hand over his. "I love the way your rough hands caress my skin. It turns me on. I can feel the strength in your hands, yet they are gentle with me."

She took another sip of the bourbon while placing Bobby's hand on her breast. He gave it a little squeeze over her shirt. Laura smiled over the rim of her glass.

"No, really, Laura. Why me?"

Laura's face turned serious. "Well, Bobby. I didn't really like you at first."

Bobby started to speak, but Laura interrupted him. "And you didn't really like me, either."

Bobby shook his head, taking another sip of his bourbon.

"You are a challenge, Bobby. I hope that doesn't sound crass. You are a challenge. There are times I still don't like you," Laura said, putting her hand up to stop Bobby from speaking again. "And I know there are times you still don't like me, either."

Bobby shook his head again and took another sip.

"But I like a good challenge, Bobby," she said, moving in closer and placing his hand back on her breast. He gave it a harder squeeze.

"Are you trying to seduce me, Miss Lucas?"

"Of course, I'm trying to seduce you."

Bobby gulped the rest of his bourbon and took a deep inhale. Laura then gulped down the rest of her drink. "Whew," she said, blowing out her breath. "Don't light a match near me."

"Yeah."

Bobby took Laura's hand and they both went into the bedroom.

When they awoke, it was late in the afternoon. Bobby stretched in his king bed. Laura rolled over, reaching for Bobby.

"You are very distracting, Laura," he said.

Laura smiled a sleepy smile. "In a good way, I hope."

"It's a good thing I've got loyal employees working for me. They can do everything without me. But I don't like not being around to do the work with them."

"I'm not stopping you from doing what you need to do."

"Laura, you know that's not true. As I said, you are very distracting." He reached over and kissed Laura. "I've got to get up and at least do the evening chores with my men."

"Can I stay here to take a shower?"

Bobby hesitated, then shook his head. "Sure."

"If you don't want me to stay, I'll go back to the hotel," she said, angry. She sat up in the bed and began to look for her clothes.

"Don't be that way, Laura. I just know if you're here when I get back, I'll get distracted again."

"You make that sound like a bad thing. If you don't want me to be so distracting, as you say, I'll go back to the hotel. Then I won't distract you."

By now, Laura was grabbing her clothes and dressing quickly, pissed off that Bobby wanted her out of his home.

"Laura," he said, reaching for her arm. "Stop it. I didn't say you shouldn't stay."

Bobby sighed. "Goddammit, why do you have to be so beautiful and so aggravating?"

Laura gave Bobby a tight smile. "Just the way I am, I guess."

She shook free of his arm and headed toward the front door. "Goodbye, Bobby. Hope you aren't too distracted to do your chores."

Laura drove her rental car back to her hotel, once again angry at Bobby. Why did he have to say the wrong thing that just made her so mad at him? It's like he was doing it intentionally, she thought.

She parked and went up to her room, then thought to check her voicemails. There was a message from Lee Adams and a missed call from Kyle Quitman, but Quitman hadn't left a message.

Laura wondered why he had called. She texted Quitman, explaining she was sorry she'd missed his call. Was there anything he needed? she asked.

When Laura didn't get a response right away, she undressed to take a hot shower. She was still feeling chilled, even after the hot sex with Bobby.

Laura stood under the shower for about a half hour, then dressed in a warm sweater and jeans. She wondered if she could turn the thermostat of her room up. She tried, but it wouldn't go higher than 76 degrees.

Laura looked in the closets and found a heavier blanket and put that on the bed as well as the thicker comforter.

She finally decided to climb into bed to see if she could get warmer. Just then she heard a text message come through on her phone.

Kyle asked how events were going at the winery and was there an update on the arson investigation. Laura had no idea whether there was an update because she hadn't called the fire marshal's office that day for an update, so she just told him there was no update, but she would call again tomorrow.

He also asked how much longer Laura expected to be out in California. Laura said she was close to getting one article in a magazine and had sent press releases to other media. The biggest thing she was working on was updating the website.

Couldn't she do that from Atlanta? he texted.

She could. Did he want her to return to Atlanta?

No, he texted. He wanted her to stay out for another week. He'd pay her another $10,000 and he wanted daily updates on the arson case. If it was unresolved after that week, she should come back to Atlanta.

Laura agreed and thanked Kyle for the opportunity to keep working on the arson crisis. She signed off with Quitman and felt relief and dread. She was ready to return to her own bed, her own city, but she realized she dreaded leaving Bobby.

As much as he was a complete pain in her ass, he was also a very good lover. She liked having sex with him. Laura wondered how he would take her leaving. Would he miss her or was she just a temporary good time for him, too?

Laura dug further under the covers and quickly fell asleep.

She awoke to the sound of her cellphone ringing. Disoriented, she answered sleepily, "Hello?"

"Laura, it's Bobby."

"Bobby?"

"I need your help. The police are here at my house and at my office. They are searching everything."

"What? Why?"

"They are questioning me about the arson again. They have a search warrant."

Laura suddenly felt an adrenaline rush though her body and felt alert. "Don't say anything. Call your attorney."

"My attorney?"

"Yes, your attorney. Whoever represented you for the sale of the winery."

"He isn't a criminal attorney. He was a tax attorney."

"Can he recommend someone? Jesus. Call him and ask!" Laura said, practically shouting. "And I'll be there as soon as I can. Don't say anything to the police without an attorney representing you."

Laura hung up and climbed out of bed. She was glad she was still wearing clothes, although her shirt was wrinkled and her hair was messy. She grabbed her comb and tried to pull it through her thick black hair. Finally, she just shook her head, hoping that her hair wouldn't look too bad.

Laura got to the winery as soon as she could without speeding through the winding roads. The last thing she wanted was a speeding ticket. She dreaded the call she'd have to make to Kyle Quitman if Bobby was arrested.

Laura rushed into Bobby's house, not even knocking on the front door.

Bobby saw her and hugged her hard. "I'm glad you're here," he whispered. "I just need you here."

"I'm here. But I'm not an attorney. Did you call about one?"

"Yes. The tax attorney gave me a name. I'll call if I need her."

"Don't you think you should call her now?"

"The tax attorney said not to call unless the police actually talk about arresting me."

"And they aren't arresting you?"

"No, Laura, they are not arresting me because I'm not guilty! I didn't set the fire!"

"OK, OK. Don't get so uptight."

"How can you say don't get uptight? I didn't do it! And it seems like you don't even believe me," Bobby said, turning away from Laura.

"I do believe you, Bobby. This is just so crazy. Why are the police questioning you?"

"I don't know! They have gone through this house and they are going through the office. They've torn up the office files! I'll never get those back in order. And they've taken my laptop. My laptop!"

"Those files were not in any kind of order, Bobby," Laura said, trying to lighten the mood.

Bobby ran his hands through his brown hair, exasperated by what was happening. "This isn't funny, Laura. The police think I'm a suspect. I don't know what to do."

"What does the warrant say? What are they looking for?"

Bobby walked over to the piece of paper on the table and began to read "propellants, solvents, flammable liquids." He threw the paper back down on the table. "Flammable liquids! This is a working farm! Of course, there are flammable liquids. We buy kerosene, propane, gasoline, all of it."

Laura walked back to Bobby and held him again in a hug. "I'm here. I think you should call the attorney and at least tell her what is happening and what the police are looking for. And tell her what you just told me. She can guide you."

"OK, but don't leave, OK?"

"I'll stay right here. Do you have a bottle of that reserve Cabernet?"

"It's over there," Bobby said, pointing to the top kitchen cabinet. "Do you really need a drink now?"

"I'm going to open it, pour it into that decanter you have, and let it breathe while you call the attorney. When you get off the phone, I think we are both going to need a drink."

The police finally left around nine o'clock that night, taking boxes of papers, other documents and Bobby's laptop with them. They wrote out a receipt of the items taken and gave them to Bobby but did not look closely to see what they took. He also didn't know what they wanted with whatever they took. They also didn't tell him if he was about to be arrested. They just told him not to leave the area.

Bobby was exhausted when they left. He felt on edge, a tense ball of nerves.

Laura handed him a large glass of the Cabernet and poured a large one for herself but pulled Bobby into the living room and sat him down in his chair. She began massaging his neck and shoulders.

"God, you are so tight."

"You think?"

Laura dug hard into his shoulders, trying to work the tension out of them. Then she turned to his neck, making him bend his head forward so she could move her hands around the nape of his neck.

"That feels good."

"We need a little warmth to help loosen those tight muscles," she said. "Tell me how to light the fireplace."

"I'll do it," he said, standing up and placing his wineglass on the side table.

"Bobby, just tell me how to do it," she said

"I've got to get some wood. I'll be right back," he said, walking out the side door. He returned shortly with an armful of wood.

He stacked most of it next to the fireplace but laid several of the cut wood in on the grate. He stuffed some newspaper under the wood and lit a fireplace match. The paper caught quickly and soon the fire had caught.

Bobby reached back to the end table and grabbed his wine, then stood in front of the fireplace. Laura came and stood beside him.

They both stood in front of the fire and sipped their wine in silence. The fire seemed to transfix them both.

"I'm glad you came. I'm glad you're here tonight," he said, his voice low. "I need you."

"I'll always be here when you need me, Bobby. Kyle told me today I can stay another week. But when I call him to tell him the police were here, he'll probably let me stay longer."

Bobby's eyes got wide. "You'll tell him the police were here? Why would you do that?"

Laura turned to Bobby, looking in his eyes. "I've got to tell him. I'm working for him, same as you. But I won't throw you under the bus. And if he thinks there might be a crisis, I'm sure he'll let me stay longer."

"You're leaving in a week?"

"That's the deal I have with Kyle right now. He's only authorized me — and is only paying me — for another week."

"Shit. I don't want you to go," Bobby said, pulling Laura close.

"Bobby, right now, I'm not going anywhere."

"I want you to stay forever," Bobby whispered in her hair.

"I can't stay forever, Bobby. But I can stay right now," she said, taking his hand and pulling him into the bedroom.

Chapter 18

Laura and Bobby awoke to the sound of Bobby's phone ringing. Bobby got up in the early light and reached for his phone on the bedroom dresser. He looked at the number and didn't recognize it. He thought about letting it go to voicemail, but since the police had been at his house and Star 1, he thought about answering it.

"Hello?"

"Mr. Pierce?"

"Yes? "

"This is Beth Reese. I'm a reporter with the Napa Valley Register. I'd like to talk to you about the recent arson at your winery. I understand the police were at your winery yesterday?"

Bobby nudged Laura to make sure she was awake.

"Ah, I really don't have a comment."

Then he mouthed to Laura it was a reporter on the line and she was asking about the arson.

Laura reached over, her breasts uncovered by the sheets, and took the cellphone from Bobby.

"Hello, who is this?" Laura asked, pulling the sheet up to cover herself in the cool bedroom.

"Who is this?" Beth asked.

"This is Laura Lucas. I'm Bobby Pierce's public relations specialist. And to whom am I speaking?"

Bobby raised his eyebrows. Laura was all business now.

"This is Beth Reese. I'm a reporter for the Napa Valley Register. I want to speak to Mr. Pierce."

"Well, Miss Reese, you are going to have to speak to me. I represent Mr. Pierce in this matter and the winery don't have a statement right now."

"But the police were out at the winery yesterday, correct?"

"Correct."

"And they are looking at Mr. Pierce as a suspect in the arson at the winery, correct?"

"Incorrect. We are cooperating fully with the arson investigation and this was simply an investigation into that inquiry."

"But the police questioned Mr. Pierce," she interrupted.

"As the police have questioned others in the inquiry, Miss Reese. Mr. Pierce is not a suspect for the arson at his own winery. We are cooperating fully. We want the arsonist brought to justice. This has caused damage and harm to the winery. And you can quote me on that."

Laura hung up on the reporter before she could ask another question. She handed Bobby's cellphone back to him. "Don't answer any more calls if you don't know the number."

"I can't do that, Laura. I have a business to run," he said, affronted by her suggestion. "I get calls from suppliers and distributors all the time. I can't just not answer my phone."

"Well then redirect those calls to me. I'll handle any media questions for you. If that reporter has sniffed out that the police were here, you can bet others will be calling, too, if not showing up with their live trucks."

"Live trucks?" Bobby asked as he got dressed.

Laura dressed quickly as well. She knew it was about to be a long day. "You know, those satellite trucks so they can do a live feed from the winery here. You might want to post one of your workers – what about that Walker fellow – down at the beginning of the driveway to stop them from coming up to do those live feeds. That might not be the kind of publicity this winery wants."

"Oh, shit. Too late," he said, peeking out the front door as a TV news van pulled up next to the office.

Laura looked over his arm to see the KGO logo on the side of the van. "What network is KGO?" she asked.

"No idea. I don't watch much TV up here, except for baseball. Signals aren't great. Should I go out there?"

"No. Stay right here. You're not in the office today. Let me finish getting dressed and I'll go out and speak with them."

Laura finished getting dressed, put a bit of makeup on and attempted to style her hair. She didn't have time to shower and blow it dry to make it look the way she wanted. "How do I look?" she asked as she was ready to step out of the house.

"Like a woman who is going to take on the world."

"I'm not taking on the world, Bobby Pierce, just the news media."

"Go get 'em," he said, before giving her a deep kiss.

"Bobby, you're going to mess up my lipstick."

Bobby kissed her again.

"You keep doing that and I won't want to leave the house."

Bobby smiled. "Well, hurry back."

"Don't let them see you. Stay back from the windows. I don't know how pushy these TV reporters here in Napa can be. Some of the ones in Atlanta are sharks."

Laura stepped out of the house and walked over to the TV reporter, who was setting up his camera. "May I help you?" she asked.

The man turned, surprised to see her. "Do you work here? I'm looking for Bobby Pierce, the owner."

"Mr. Pierce isn't here today. I'm Laura Lucas. I do publicity for Star 1. Perhaps I can help you."

"Mrs. Lucas, I'm Daniel Norris, an investigative reporter with KGO. We got a tip that police were out here with a search warrant, looking for evidence in the arson case. We understand the police are about to make an arrest."

"That's news to me, and I do the publicity here. Where did you get this tip? From the police?"

"No, we got an anonymous tip, but it's from a reliable source."

"Can't be that reliable if it's not true," Laura purred.

"Well, were the police out here, Mrs. Lucas?"

"It's Miss Lucas, Daniel. Mrs. Lucas is my mother. To answer your question, yes. The fire investigators have been out here several times during their investigation. We have been cooperating fully with the investigation. The fire caused damage to the winery and the vines. We want whoever is responsible to be brought to justice."

"Can I get a shot of the damage? Will you take me to it and do an interview there? You're sure Mr. Pierce isn't here?" Daniel asked, looking around.

"I'm sure Mr. Pierce isn't here, but I think that I can take you down to see the damaged area. I just need to go back into the house to get my jacket. It's chilly today."

"It's chilly every day in mid-June."

"Well, I wouldn't know. I'm from Atlanta, where it's hot and humid this time of year. I'll be right back."

Laura walked in the front door and shooed Bobby back. "Get away from the door," she hissed. "I told him you weren't here today."

"What did you say?"

"I told him exactly what I told the newspaper reporter who called you. I said we are cooperating fully. He wants a live shot down where the fire was. I'm going to take him down there."

"He's not bringing that van down there is he?"

"I won't let him. I'll make him carry his camera, set it up, do the interview and get rid of him."

"OK. Just don't let him drive that thing down there. It might get stuck in the mud."

Laura smiled. "Well, I should let him drive it down there then, just to see if that would happen."

"Don't you dare," Bobby said, his face dark.

"I'm just teasing. I need my jacket. Stay out of sight."

Laura stepped outside again with her jacket and saw Daniel Norris trying to look in the window.

"I'm right here, Daniel. No need to peek in the window."

Daniel gave her a sheepish grin. "I thought I heard someone talking."

"Nope. Just me. Now, I'm going to have to ask you to carry your camera down to the site. Mr. Pierce has told me time and again no vehicles other than ATVs are to go down into the vineyard."

"Do you have an ATV we can use? This camera and the tripod are heavy."

"Sorry. I don't have the key to one. Let's go, it's not all that far," she said, turning and walking the path down toward the far end.

Daniel put the tripod over his shoulder and carried the camera and dutifully began to follow her but turned back to look toward the house. He thought he saw the curtain at the window move.

"Ah, Miss Lucas, I think someone is in that house," he said, pointing back.

"Why do you say that?" she asked, sweetly.

"I just saw the curtain move."

"Daniel, it's probably the cat. I can't keep that cat off the windowsill. It's a wonder the curtains aren't torn to shreds. Now come on. The light ought to be perfect this morning for the shot."

Laura put her arm through Daniel's and led him away from the house. Inside, she was seething. Hadn't she told Bobby to stay away from the window? She needed him to lay low until she could find out who the anonymous tipster was and whether the police really were about to make an arrest. And she needed to know whether the person about to be arrested was him.

"So, how long have you been a TV reporter?" she asked as they walked down the path.

"I've been here for about two years. I was lucky to get this job. My last job was out in Kansas City. San Francisco is a much bigger market."

"Well, isn't Kansas City a big market?"

"Bigger than my first job in Topeka, Kansas. I reported on farm futures there. That was an ABC affiliate too. KTKA. I don't miss that place."

"And the station where you are now is an ABC station?" she asked.

"Yes. I went from Topeka to Kansas City to here, all with ABC. My dream is to one day work for the network," Daniel said, starting to perspire on his upper lip. "Is it much farther?"

"Not much, we go left just down here. You said you got a tip about the arson?"

"Yeah. Said we should check it out. That it might be an inside job."

"We'll I don't think that is true. Bobby Pierce sold the majority interest of Star 1 to an investor. Unless there is a winery worker with a grudge, I can't see someone here starting the fire. The investor gets nothing if we can't produce wine. And with burnt vines, we won't produce as much wine."

"Oh, I didn't realize that. Can I talk to the investor? Is he here locally?"

"He's in Austin, Texas. He has several companies that he has invested in."

"Can I get his name?"

"I'll print out the release when we get back to the office. Here we are," she said, pointing out the charred vines and burned trellises that had once held them.

"This doesn't look that bad," Daniel said, disappointment on his face.

"We were very lucky the county fire department got here so quickly. It could have been far worse. But it's about 30 acres, maybe less."

"Yes, I see."

Daniel sighed. He picked up his camera and began to film the ruined vines for B-roll. Then he set up his tripod and got Laura to stand in front of the camera.

"I'm just going to ask you some questions. Just look at me when you answer them. Don't look straight at the camera."

Laura wanted to roll her eyes. This wasn't her first on-camera interview.

Daniel asked the same questions as before and Laura responded with as little information as she could give him.

Daniel tried to ask his questions in a different way, but Laura continued to answer evasively.

"Miss Lucas, I think we're done here," Daniel said, clearly frustrated he wasn't getting the big scoop he thought he'd been tipped off about.

"I hope you have everything you need. I'll send you the press release when I get back to my laptop. Do you have a card?"

As they walked up the path back to the house and office, Daniel stopped, put the tripod and camera down and pulled a business card out of his jacket pocket and handed it to her.

Then he hoisted the tripod over his shoulder, picked up the camera and continued the walk back up the path.

When they got to his news van, Daniel put the tripod in the back and placed the camera in a large case into a foam form that enveloped it snuggly.

"Be sure to email me that release, OK?"

"Of course, I'll do it as soon as I get to my laptop."

"Isn't your laptop in the house?"

"Actually, it's at the Hampton Inn. That's where I'm staying while I'm out here."

Daniel looked at her, puzzled. "Well, send it to me soon. I'll have this on the noon news."

"I'll head back to my hotel right now."

"Thanks."

Laura waved to Daniel as he pulled the van onto the driveway and headed toward the main road. She turned to the house and saw a twitch at the curtained window.

She entered the house and hissed at Bobby. "I told you to stay away from the window. Daniel saw you and I had to tell him it was a cat in the window."

"He's gone?"

"He's gone, but he said the newsroom got a tip that an arrest is about to be made. Bobby, is there anything you aren't telling me?"

"Laura, I did not have anything to do with this!" he said, raising his voice. "Why don't you believe me?"

"OK. OK. Don't get so touchy. I've got to call Kyle and give him an update and warn him he may get a call from Daniel."

"Who's Daniel?"

"That reporter," she said, looking down at the business card in her hand. "Daniel Norris."

"We're on a first name basis with him now?" Bobby said, irritated.

"Oh, I made him call me Miss Lucas. I'd never get familiar with a news reporter," she said, making a face of disgust.

Bobby grabbed Laura by the arm. "Listen, we need to be clear on this. I did not start that fire."

Laura looked down at Bobby's hand on her arm. "Let go of me."

Bobby dropped his hand. "Sorry, I didn't mean to hurt you. I just want to make it clear I didn't start that fire. I was with you all night that night in case you forgot."

"I didn't forget. I just don't think you are telling me the whole truth."

"Why don't you believe me?"

"I'm good at reading when someone is being untruthful, Bobby. My brother, Rico, was a very good study in — shall we say — being deceitful. I learned from the best."

"So, you think I'm lying."

"I'm saying I don't think you are telling me the whole truth. I can't put my finger on it. I don't believe you started the fire. But I can't help feeling you had something to do with it. I'm not entirely sure why. It's just a gut feeling. And I always follow my gut."

Bobby's eyes flared with anger. "I had nothing to do with this, and I don't appreciate your accusing me of a crime." Bobby went silent, then said in a low voice. "I think you should leave. Take your stuff and don't come back. If you don't trust me, I can't trust you."

Laura's lips tightened and she nodded her head. "Fine. Give me just a few minutes to collect my things."

Laura stuffed most of her clothes in a small bag and walked out of Bobby's house without saying another word.

Laura was back at her hotel, on the phone with Kyle Quitman, giving him an update on the morning's events.

Quitman was unhappy.

"You were supposed to generate good publicity out there! Now Bobby's office and house are being searched? The winery's paperwork and Bobby's laptop was taken? The media is out there? The winery is going to be on the evening news? This is a disaster!"

"We don't know what the police have found, if anything. They left the search warrant, so we know they were looking for any receipts of 'solvents, flammable liquids, propellants.' I'm surmising they suspect Bobby of the arson. He insists he did not start the fire and that he had nothing to do with it."

"How can you know he didn't start the fire, Laura? How can you know that for certain?"

"Well, I was with him the night the fire started."

"What you do mean you were with him?"

"I was with him the night the fire started," she said, trying to be evasive.

"You mean you're sleeping with him?"

"Well…"

"Marc Linder warned me about you. He warned me!" Kyle interrupted.

"What the hell did Marc say?"

"That I could not trust you. That you tried to break up him and Ravyn. You know that didn't work. They are still together. Although keeping them together cost me quite a bit, thanks to you."

"What do you mean?"

"Never mind. Just take care of this or I'm not paying you one dime. Not the retainer and not the commission. Do you understand me?"

"I understand."

"And stop sleeping with Bobby! Jesus! I can't believe you!"

"Hey, stay out of my private life. I don't tell you who to sleep with."

"I'm married, Laura. I sleep with my wife."

"Well, good for you, Kyle. I'm single. I can sleep with any man I want. Remember what it was like to be single? It's fun."

"Fun? I expect you to be professional, Laura, not acting like a teenager."

"I've been very discrete."

"I should hope so!"

"I want a daily report from now on. I want every scrap of publicity that's out there, good or bad. I'm regretting making this purchase."

"I will send you everything I can find."

Kyle hung up without saying goodbye. Laura could feel the tension in her body rise. She felt nervous energy coursing through her body. She needed to burn off this energy. Normally, she did it with sex.

But sex with Bobby was out, given his throwing her out of his house and telling her not to come back. She wondered if she should call Lee.

Laura took out her cellphone and pushed his contact number.

"Hello, Laura. What can I do for you?" he asked.

"I was wondering if we could look at those videos again. Since I now have access to the Star 1 website, thanks to your guy, I might add, I'd like to load a few of your videos."

"Would you like me to come to your hotel?"

"I'm happy to come to you. You have the editing equipment at your house, just in case we need to change anything."

"Sure. I'll be there around four o'clock today."

"That's great. Should I bring some takeout in case we work late?"

"How late do you think this will take?"

"I'm not sure. Do you have plans tonight?"

"No."

"Well, I'll go ahead and get takeout. Anywhere in particular I should get it?"

"There's a good Indian place in town. Do you like Indian?"

"Love it. There's a great place at home in Buckhead near my condo."

"Buckhead? I thought you lived in Atlanta."

"I do. Buckhead is an area in the city of Atlanta. What's the address of the place here? And any favorites?"

Lee gave her the address and requested chicken tikka masala with brown rice.

Laura picked up their orders, including extra naan bread and some samosas, both vegetable and lamb.

She pulled up to Lee's house about shortly after four o'clock, taking the takeout bags out of her car, which now smelled like curry. She wondered if she should leave the car windows open to air it out. She decided she should. She didn't want to drive home later tonight with a car that smelled of Indian food.

Laura sort of kicked the front door with her boots since her hands were full. Lee answered and took one of the bags from her.

"You must have gotten extra."

"I got some samosas as well, vegetarian and meat."

"This smells great. Thanks for getting it. You expensed it, I'm sure."

"Well, I intend to. This is a working dinner."

"Of course," he nodded stiffly. "Shall we eat first or get right to work?"

"The food is hot. Let's eat now. I didn't have lunch, so I'm ready to eat."

"Sounds great. Should I get some wine?"

"That Chardonnay you have would be great with this food, don't you think?"

"I think you are right," Lee said, going to the small wine cellar in his kitchen and pulling out a perfectly chilled bottle of Chardonnay."

Laura went to Lee's kitchen cabinets and began searching for some plates. When she found them, she grabbed two, then found wine glasses and cutlery.

"Where are the napkins?" she asked.

"In the drawer over there," Lee pointed to a drawer near the sink.

Laura found the napkins and set the table. Then she began opening the takeout containers, putting spoons in them. She pulled out plastic cutlery from the bags as well.

"I'd rather have the real thing than these things," she said, throwing the plasticware on the table.

They sat down and enjoyed an early dinner. The first bottle of wine was consumed before they finished their meal and Lee opened another. They were done about an hour and half later.

Laura placed her napkin on her plate when Lee asked, "Why are you really here tonight, Laura?"

"I told you. I'd like to load some of those videos on the website. I have the admin privileges now. With what's going on at the winery, I need some good marketing."

"What's going on at the winery?"

"Oh nothing. It's just with the arson investigation going on, everyone's on edge."

"You mean, Bobby Pierce is on edge because the police have been there with a search warrant."

"How did you know?"

"Napa really is a small community, Laura. I knew about it shortly after the police arrived."

"Who at the winery is your snitch?"

Lee smiled. "Now that would be telling."

Laura frowned. She didn't like that someone at the winery was spreading gossip about what was going on there.

"Don't worry, Laura. I didn't tell anyone else. The winery is my client, after all, I do have loyalty to my clients."

"That's good to know."

"So why are you here?"

"I can't have dinner with a client?"

"I don't think you are here to just have dinner. Am I the dessert?" he asked, secretly hoping he was.

"I think there is a small bag of Gulab jamun in here," Laura said, reaching for the white plastic bag and pulling out a white paper bag. She ripped it open and handed it to Lee, who pulled a small sticky pastry out.

Lee tried to hide his disappointment at her changing the subject as he popped the traditional dessert in his mouth.

He chewed and swallowed, saying, "It's good. They do a good Gulab jamun there."

Laura bit daintily into the spongy dessert then wiped her mouth, the syrup that was soaked in it dripped from her lip.

"They certainly do."

"Shall we get started on the videos?"

"Sure, let's just put away the dishes."

They cleared the table and Lee loaded the dishes into the dishwasher. He loaded some other dishes, then started it. The slight whooshing indicated it had started.

They moved into Lee's video editing suite and went over the winery video. The overhead camera from the drone created a sweeping vista of the vines, fortunately for them, before the fire.

"I really like this part," Laura said, pointing out the introductory part of the video. It then cut away to various photos from the winery, including the event space with just tables and chairs, set up as if it were ready for an event. Then the video included some photos of the models at the event space and out in the fields. Lee had included a slideshow of the wines.

"I'd kind of like the order of the photos to change, though," she said.

Lee stopped the video and rewound it, stopping it at the end of the introductory footage from the drone. "Sure. What order do you want them in?"

Laura outlined that she like the event space photos, but wanted the models interspersed with other event space shots, shots of the wine, then the photos of the models out in the vineyard.

"I can do that," Lee said. "I can probably do that tomorrow."

"That would be great. Then I can upload it."

"Is that it?" He asked.

"Well, I'd like another glass of that wine, if there is any left," she said.

"I can open another bottle."

"Did we drink both bottles?"

"I think there was a little left, but we should open a fresh bottle. Whatever is left will be warm. We want it at the right temperature. Wine is truly best at the right temperature."

"Oh, of course," Laura said, shaking her head.

"Let's sit out on the back patio. I can start a fire in the fire pit."

"Oh, that will be lovely. We can watch the sunset."

"Laura, the sun won't set for a couple more hours."

"Oh? I thought we were in the editing suite for several of hours. Guess I lost track of time."

Lee smiled. "Well, sunset will be in a couple of hours."

"It will be nice to see the sunset."

"Indeed."

Lee got another bottle of the Chardonnay and they moved out to the patio. Lee pulled some wood from a wood pile and started the fire pit.

Laura remembered to bring her jacket with her and sat in the chaise lounge, comfortable in front of the fire.

Lee poured the wine into her glass, filling it three-quarters of the way.

"Oh, a generous portion tonight. Thanks."

Lee poured himself a similar glass.

They chatted amicably, asking each other about their early careers, laughing about early mistakes they made.

"I was supposed to take these gorgeous sunset photos off Catalina Island for a magazine and I forgot to take off the lens cap!" Lee said, laughing. Laura laughed right along with him.

"Oh, early in my career I was working for an agency and got a senior account, and I made a horrible typo. I misspelled the name of the company! It went out in a press release. Thank God they didn't fire me. They could have. They just put me on a very junior account. I had to work my way back up."

The sun began to set and they both got quiet. Lee's back patio faced west, they could see the light turn pink and then orange before the sun went behind some trees.

"That was lovely," Laura said.

"You're lovely. I like you. I'm very attracted to you, Laura," Lee said, suddenly serious.

"I like you, too," Laura replied, but suddenly cautious.

"Would you like to stay over tonight?"

"Would you like me to?"

"Only if you want to," Lee said. "I certainly won't force you to stay. But I'm hoping you might have an itch I can scratch tonight."

Laura laughed out loud, her laughter echoing out from the patio and into the woods in the backyard. "Well, Lee, I believe you can scratch my itch tonight."

Chapter 19

Laura's cellphone vibrated at seven o'clock the next morning. She hadn't meant to spend the entire night with Lee. She thought she'd go home after they'd had sex, but with the Indian food she'd eaten and all the wine she'd drunk, she fell into a sound sleep shortly after she'd climaxed.

Besides, the bed was so warm as she snuggled next to Lee's body.

After she had fully awakened, Laura could hear Lee snoring beside her. Laura was surprised he didn't hear her phone vibrate, although she'd turned her phone's ringtone off the night before when they were out on the back patio.

Laura wondered if she could quietly get up, get dressed and leave before Lee awoke. Wouldn't be the first time she'd crept out of a man's bedroom without saying goodbye. She was certain it wouldn't be the last time, either.

Laura slid out of bed as quietly as she could, gathered her clothes and crept into the living room. She dressed in there, then found the guest bathroom. She was nervous about flushing the toilet but didn't think she could wait until she got back to her hotel.

She had her hand on the door when she heard Lee's voice. "Where are you going?"

Laura spun around, surprised. "I'm going back to my hotel to shower and get breakfast. Busy day today. And you'll have a busy day, too, if you plan to get the video re-edited for me."

"I can fix your breakfast here," he said.

"Thanks, but I've got work to do."

"This early in the morning?"

"Lee, thank you for your hospitality last night," Laura said, unlocking the front door and heading to her car. She turned to see his disappointed face at the door. "I'll call you later, OK?"

Laura waved her hand as she got in her car and she saw Lee give a half wave before turning back into his house and closing the door with a bang.

Laura would like to say she felt guilty about Lee, but she didn't like to lie to herself. Lee was a nice distraction and an OK lover. Lee got the job done.

But Lee wasn't Bobby. Bobby was a very good lover. Maybe even a great lover. What disappointed her the most was the way she and Bobby had ended their relationship. With just a week left to stay in Napa, she'd rather be in Bobby's bed.

Laura parked in the hotel parking lot and went straight for coffee. Once she'd gotten her coffee, she looked over her options for breakfast. Some sort of breakfast burrito with egg and cheese. She saw a small bowl with salsa in it. Laura thought that was likely the only way to eat the burrito. Laura considered going out for breakfast but didn't have the energy.

Laura put a breakfast burrito on her paper plate, took several slices of bacon and put wheat bread in the communal toaster. A few seconds later she sat in the breakfast area and was dipping her burrito in salsa.

Laura fixed another cup of coffee with lots of sugar before going up to her room. She finished her coffee before going to take her shower.

Laura dried and styled her thick black hair, dressed more meticulously today. She was going to visit some of the TV stations and newspapers, as well as the fire department to get any update in person. She knew that would please Kyle Quitman that she was putting herself in front of those that either had the information or wanted the information.

She called to make an appointment for the fire department inspector and was happy to get in a little after one o'clock in that afternoon. That would leave plenty of time to make the rounds at the local TV stations and newspapers to make the early news. She was irritated she couldn't just call a press conference to be held at the winery, which would have been much easier.

Damn you, Bobby, she thought. I need to be on that property! How else am I supposed to do my job? It was a huge mistake to come out here. I wonder if I can just leave, she thought.

Laura began to think her actions through. Kyle Quitman wouldn't pay her and would probably make it difficult to get other clients.

Laura sighed. She would have to do as best she could and stay in Napa for another week. But she wouldn't stay longer. She would make sure of that.

Laura arrived at the Napa Valley Fire Marshal's office shortly before one o'clock. She sat down in the small lobby. The padded wooden chair reminded her of government furniture. Out of date magazines were on the coffee table, most of them related to firefighting and forestry management. She flipped through them out of boredom.

After about 20 minutes, Laura was led back to a drab office with the name Sgt. Rebecca Gladwell on the door plate.

Gladwell stood, walked around her desk and shook Laura's hand, then gestured for her to sit down on another padded wooden chair. Laura looked down quickly and could see coffee stains on it. She sat down anyway.

"What can I do for you, Miss Lucas?" Gladwell asked.

"I'd like to know if there are any updates to the arson case at Star 1 Winery. I'm planning to give the investor of the winery an update later today and to speak to the media."

"We don't have anything to update," Gladwell said. "It's an open investigation and we're still investigating. I'm sorry I can't help you with anything more."

"Is Bobby Pierce a suspect? I ask because he is the manager at the winery. My client, the investor in the winery, is concerned whether he should keep Bobby in that position," Laura said. Laura was lying to the fire investigator but wanted to know if Bobby was about to be arrested.

"I don't know what to tell you, Miss Lucas, nor do I know what to advise your client. That is for your client to decide. I can't say whether Mr. Pierce is a suspect, nor whether he isn't a suspect. This is an open investigation and I'm not at liberty to say one way or the other."

Gladwell stood, reaching out to shake Laura's hand. Laura stood as well. "Thank you for stopping by Miss Lucas. I have your card should I need to reach you. Sorry I couldn't be of more help."

"Well, I thank you for your time, Sgt. Gladwell. I do appreciate it. I think I can see myself out."

Laura turned toward the door and Gladwell followed her out until they had reached the front door of the office building. Laura left and found where she'd parked her car.

She sat in the car and wondered what she would do with not having any new information. She could barely meet with the media and give press releases with nothing to tell.

Laura's whole afternoon was now shot. She was glad she hadn't set up the meetings at the TV stations. They would have laughed her out of the newsrooms.

Instead, Laura would call Kyle with the news that there was no news. That probably would not make him happy. She was growing weary this afternoon and was glad her time in Napa was ending. She was ready to get back to Atlanta.

Laura returned to her hotel room, grabbing a cup of coffee on the way up. She was grateful the hotel always had coffee in the lobby.

She threw her handbag on the freshly made bed and pulled off her cowboy boots. Laura wiggled her toes to get the circulation going in her feet.

She contemplated laying down on her hotel bed for a nap, but it was too late in the day for that. Laura was afraid if she tried to nap now, she'd wake up in the middle of the night and be unable to fall back asleep.

Honestly, the only time she'd been sleeping well on this trip is when she'd had great sex. Well, she wasn't going to have great sex with Bobby any time soon. She'd have to settle for more mediocre sex with Lee.

Laura picked up her cellphone, ready to call Lee. Could she use the excuse to see the video again? She thought that request was probably wearing thin. Lee would see she just wanted him for sex. Not that she thought he minded.

Instead, she called Kyle Quitman and told him there was no update on the arson investigation and that she'd asked if an arrest was imminent but got a non-answer from the investigator.

"Well, wrap up what you can by the end of this week and come back to Atlanta," Kyle said. "I have another project for you. But you have to promise me you won't sleep with anyone at the business."

"I promise. What's the job?"

"I've purchased a chain of restaurants — all over metro Atlanta — and I want you to do the publicity for it."

"What's the chain of restaurants?" Laura asked, curious. She'd worked with a few of the independent restaurant groups in Atlanta.

"Seventh Heaven Restaurant Group. You know them?"

"I've worked with Simon Beck, one of the partners. They sold the restaurant group to you? I didn't think they'd ever sell. There are three partners."

"They want to expand and don't have the capital to do that. I'm now a fourth partner. As part of the deal, I make some of the financial calls."

"So, I'm hired permanently?" Laura asked with hope in her voice.

"We'll discuss that when you are back in Atlanta," Kyle said. "I don't think I'll be in Atlanta for a while, but we can do a phone conference."

"I look forward to it," she said. She could barely keep the happiness out of her voice. A client! And a client with deep pockets, too.

This time, Kyle actually said goodbye before he hung up.

She remembered Simon Beck. He was quite handsome. A Gordon Ramsey kind of guy. She wasn't sure he was single. He wasn't the last time she'd dealt with him. But she'd look forward to reacquainting herself with him.

Laura felt relief wash over her. She decided she would treat herself to a nice dinner. She certainly didn't want to eat alone, so she decided to call Lee.

That was a good reason to call him. She doubted he'd turn down an invitation to a nice dinner, especially if she could expense it.

As she held the phone in her hand to call Lee, it rang and she saw Bobby's name.

"Hello? Bobby?"

"Laura, I've been arrested."

"What? Why?"

"I've been arrested for arson at the winery."

"What?" she said, her voice raising in alarm. "You told me you had nothing to do with it!" she said, angry at him.

173

"I didn't have anything to do with it!" Bobby shouted. Then he spoke in a low voice. "I'm at the police station. I need your help."

"You need an attorney, not my help. I told you to call an attorney."

"Shut up. I need you to go to my office and get the number for my attorney and call her. I think I'm going to be arraigned tomorrow morning and I'm hoping I'll get bail."

"They are keeping you overnight?"

"From what they've told me, yes. Will you please go to the office and get that number and call her? Please? I really need your help."

"I don't have the key to your office."

"Check with Walker Folks. He's got the keys."

"Walker Folks?"

"You've seen him around the winery. He's one of my main hands. I'm sure you've seen him. Ask at the winery."

"What evidence do they have against you?" she asked.

"They say they've found receipts for 'flammable liquids' in my possession. I mean, of course they'd find that. I authorize gasoline purchases and that shit all the time."

"Didn't you tell them that?"

"Of course I did," Bobby said, exasperated.

"Did the receipt have your credit card number on it?"

"No, it was paid in cash. The receipt was dated the day before the fire. But I didn't buy any that day. I buy it at the first of the month with all of my supplies."

"Tell them that!" Laura exclaimed.

"You think I didn't? They don't believe me. All they want to believe is that bogus receipt."

"OK. I'll go to the office and call your attorney. Be safe, Bobby."

"I will," Bobby said, his voice cracking.

Laura didn't want to hang up, but Bobby disconnected the call.

Laura was shocked at the turn of events. She felt betrayed by Sgt. Gladwell. She had lied to her, and Laura always prided herself with being able to tell when people were lying to her. She'd been lied to so many times.

Laura pulled her boots back on and grabbed her car keys and handbag and headed out of the hotel for Star 1 Winery.

She pulled up to the office and got out of her car. Unsurprisingly, the door was locked. She peered in but the lights were off and she couldn't see anything.

Laura began looking around for anyone to ask who, and where, was Walker Folks. The winery appeared to be deserted. A shiver ran down her body. Where was everyone? Were they all on a break? Had they heard about Bobby's arrest and quit?

She walked back toward the shed, where she'd seen men working before. Maybe they were working on equipment there. She went into the dim shed but didn't see anyone.

A stocky man in jeans and a red plaid flannel shirt stood up from behind a large tractor and came towards Laura, startling her.

"Oh!" she exclaimed. "You scared me."

"Sorry, didn't mean to do that," he said, wiping his hands on a greasy rag. "I was working on the tractor. What can I do for you? You here to see Bobby? He's not here. He went into town earlier. Don't know when he'll be back."

Laura knew instantly that he didn't know Bobby had been arrested, and that Bobby must have been arrested after being asked to go to the police station.

"I just talked to Bobby," Laura said carefully, recognizing the farm hand. "He needs something in the office, but the door is locked. He said Walker Folks would have the key. You're Walker, aren't you?"

"That's me," Folks said, extending a still dirty hand. He looked down at his hand and dropped it. "Sorry. I've been working on the tractor."

"That's alright. Do you have the key, or can you tell me where it is?"

"I think Bobby took it with him," Folks lied.

"Oh," Laura replied. The hair on the back of her neck stood on end. She knew Walker was lying. "But he said you'd have the key. I don't think he took it with him."

Folks shrugged his shoulders. "Don't know what to tell you. I don't have it. What's so important in the office?"

"Paperwork. Something to do with the insurance after the fire."

"Sorry. You'll have to wait for Bobby to come back."

"Well, since I can't wait in his office, I'll have to go back to my hotel."

"Suit yourself."

As Folks went back to working on the tractor, Laura walked back to her car. She wondered why he'd lied to her. She couldn't very well break a window to get into the office. Folks would see and hear that. She wished she knew how to pick a lock.

Laura sighed a deep sigh of regret. Rico knew how to pick a lock. She was sure he'd done it at their parents' house as a teenager when they'd locked him out after he'd missed his curfew.

She couldn't very well call a locksmith either. She wasn't the property owner.

Laura got back into her car and headed to her hotel. She prayed she could call Bobby on his cellphone and talk to him about the conversation with Walker Folks.

But his cellphone went to voicemail when she tried to call him. Laura could picture it inside some evidence locker at the police station.

Laura paced her hotel room. Should she call Kyle and tell him Bobby had been arrested? No, that might get him fired.

She wished Bobby had told her the name of his attorney. She could have looked it up and called her. She cursed Bobby. Why hadn't he listened to her? Would he be able to call her when he didn't hear from his attorney? She desperately hoped so.

Laura jumped when her cellphone rang. She could see it was Lee Adams.

"Hi, Lee, what's up?" she asked, hoping the strain she felt wasn't in her voice.

"I just wanted you to know I completed the edits of the video. Want to come over to see it?"

Laura knew what he meant by that. He wanted her to come over for sex tonight. She was too jittery to even think of having sex with Lee. And anyway, Bobby needed her.

"I'm sorry, Lee. I can't come over tonight. I've got some other things I need to do."

"Like what?"

"I need some papers in Bobby Pierce's office, but it's locked and the man who has the key can't find it."

"Where's Bobby? Why can't he get them?"

"Ah, he's out of town at the moment and he needed me to retrieve the papers and give him the information on them."

"Out of town? If he's out of town you can come over. You said you can't get into his office, right?"

"Right, but I'm going to try to see if I can't get into the office another way. He really said he needed the papers."

"What are you going to do? Pick the lock?" Lee said it to be funny, but she was contemplating how she could find someone to pick the lock.

"Ha ha. Aren't you funny? Might have to call a locksmith."

"Sounds like a lot of trouble for some paperwork," Lee said, suspicion in his voice.

"Well, I can't exactly break the door down or bust out a window," Laura said with a forced laugh. "Lee, I'm going to have to go. I've really got to figure out how to get that paperwork."

"OK. What about later? After you get the paperwork? Would you like to come over then?"

"We'll see, Lee. Thanks, I've got to go." Laura hung up before he could say another word. Damn, he was nosy, she thought. She hoped she hadn't made him too suspicious about where Bobby was.

Laura did call a locksmith just to see if she could get him to open the office. He asked a few questions and then said he'd meet her out at Star 1 Winery.

She hadn't exactly lied to Eric Hammond. She just didn't say she *was* the property owner. She did say she was representing the property owner. That seemed to satisfy him.

Hammond said he could meet her at six o'clock, but it would cost extra since it was an after-hours appointment. She said she'd give him $100 extra dollars for his trouble. Hammond said he'd be there.

Money talked, even in California, Laura thought.

Laura got to the office about 5:30 p.m. and was surprised to find the office door slightly ajar. No lights were on and she pushed the door open. "Hello?" she called out.

Walker Folks whirled around to face her.

"What are you doing here?" he sneered.

Laura stepped back. Every fiber of her body suddenly alert.

"I thought you said you didn't have the key to this office," she said. "What are *you* doing here?"

Laura could vaguely see he was carrying what looked like an old metal gasoline can in one hand. "Hey, what are you doing?"

Walker suddenly splashed her with some of the gasoline in the can and began pouring the rest of the contents on the desk and floor.

"Oh, shit! You're the one who set the fire! Help! Fire! Fire!" she began to shout.

Walker quickly crossed to her and pinned her against the wall, a hand over her mouth. It smelled of gasoline and Laura felt light-headed.

"Shut up, bitch. Shut the fuck up. I know what you're up to. I know you work for the man who bought this place."

Laura tried to knee him in the crotch, but he turned and then stepped on her foot, hard. Laura winced in pain. "You want to play games, Laura? You want to play with me?"

Laura's eyes were wide. Fear strummed through her body. She was beginning to flashback to Julio's attack on her. She suddenly bit down hard on Walker's finger.

"Fucking bitch!" he yelled, letting go of her mouth and seeing that she'd drawn blood. He drew his arm back to hit her, and her self-defense training kicked in. She parried and tried to get out of the office door, but he'd shut it. She tore at his clothing as he tried to pin her arms.

She began yelling "Fire!" again and he slapped her hard. She could feel her lip begin to bleed.

"You bitch." He shoved her hard and she lost balance, landing on the gasoline-soaked floor. "Die, bitch."

He opened the office door, turned and snapped his lighter, tossing it into the room. He closed the door, with Laura still inside. Laura could have wept when the flame went out as the lighter sailed through the air.

Walker turned when he heard a vehicle pull up to the office. Eric Hammond Locksmith was painted on the side of a white pickup truck.

"Is Laura Lucas here?" Eric asked, getting out of his truck. "I'm here to open the office. Is it open already?"

Laura began shouting "Fire! Fire!" again as loud as she could from the window of the office door. Eric looked puzzled. Walker took a swing at Eric, but Eric saw it coming. He put his arm up, blocking the blow.

Eric then grabbed a wrench and hit Walker on the shoulder, making Walker drop to the ground. Walker stood and stumbled toward the outbuildings.

"What's going on?" Eric demanded.

Laura opened the office door and flung herself at Eric. "Help me! That man attacked me and tried to set me on fire!"

"Let me call the police," Eric said, reaching for his cellphone and calling 911. "Can you talk to them?"

Laura nodded her head and took his phone, suddenly yelping in pain. She switched to her left hand and in a rush of words, she told the dispatcher she'd been attacked by Walker Folks at Star 1 Winery and he'd tried to set her on fire in the office. He was the arsonist.

"Where is the suspect now?" the dispatcher asked, dispassionately.

"I don't know. He took off. I think he's somewhere on the property. I'm afraid." And for the first time in a very long time, Laura began to cry.

In what seemed to take hours, Eric and Laura stood together in front of the office and then began to hear sirens and see flashing lights arriving at Star 1. Several police vehicles and a fire engine arrived, along with an ambulance at the rear.

A police corporal began to wave to other officers to fan out and look for Walker Folks. Laura tried to give a description as best she could. Eric filled in a little more. Another officer took Eric's statement of having been assaulted before hitting Folks with his wrench.

The police told Laura she needed to immediately get out of her gasoline-soaked clothes. They were considered a hazard.

"But I don't have any other clothes here!" she shrieked, her voice going higher in her panic.

The officer waved over the EMTs and asked for a blanket. Laura could wrap up in that.

"Do you need help with your clothes?" the female officer asked.

"My wrist. I think it's broken," Laura said, holding out her right wrist which was at an odd angle.

The officer waved over the EMTs but took Laura around to the side of a building where she helped her out of her pants and blouse. The EMTs splinted up her wrist and wrapped her in a blanket.

The EMTs then tended to Laura's lip.

"We'll need to bag your clothes for evidence. You don't have any clothes here?" the female officer asked.

Laura shook her head. "All of my clothes are back at my hotel."

"Which hotel?"

"Hampton Inn. Room 305." She handed her keycard to a young officer. "My blouses are in the closet and so are my pants. My, ah, underthings are in the right-hand drawer. The gasoline soaked through everything."

Laura could see the young officer flush, but he nodded and went back to his patrol car and left the winery.

"You won't take my boots, will you?" Laura asked. "They were expensive!"

The officer nodded, allowing Laura to keep her boots. "OK, can you take me through the events again? Why were you here at the office?"

"I was here to get the attorney's name for Bobby Pierce. You arrested him for the arson here at the winery, which he clearly didn't do."

Laura saw the female officer look up, her eyes widen, then look back down at her notepad.

"Walker Folks did it," Laura said with certainty. "He told me he didn't have the key to the office, but when I got here, he was in the office with the gas can. He threw some of it on me and then poured the rest of it on the desk and the floor. I think he was trying to destroy evidence and he was trying to lock me in. He was trying to kill me!"

Laura's voice got shrill and high when she went over the story again, the gravity of what Walker was trying to do finally sinking in.

"Calm down, Mrs. Lucas," the officer said.

"Miss Lucas. And he said 'Die, bitch' as he shoved me to the floor. Then he lit a lighter. Thank God it went out after he threw it, or I wouldn't be talking to you now." Laura's hands and body began to shake uncontrollably.

"Medic!" the officer shouted. The EMTs got a stretcher out of the ambulance and the officer helped Laura to lay down on it. "I think you are going into shock," she explained.

One EMT took her pulse then put a blood pressure cuff on her. They took out some medical bags, started an IV of fluids for her. "I think we need to bring her to the hospital for observation," another EMT said.

"No!" Laura shouted. She tried to sit up, but an EMT started to hold her down. "I'm not going. I'm refusing medical treatment!"

"Miss Lucas, I think. . . ." the female officer started to say.

"I don't care what you think! I'm refusing medical treatment. I'm not going to the hospital!"

"OK, let's calm down," the EMT said in his best soothing voice. "I think you should get checked out. I think you are going into shock. What happened to you is certainly traumatic."

At that moment, an officer came up to the office with Walker Folks in handcuffs.

"Can you identify this man?" he asked Laura.

"That's the asshole who tried to kill me!" she shouted. "That's Walker Folks! The arsonist!"

Eric also confirmed Folks was the one who attempted to assault him as well.

"You fucking bitch!" Folks shouted at Laura. "I wish you had died in the fire! Then your charred body would be the only thing in that office for Bobby to find! You bitch! Bobby never should have sold this place!"

The officer began to drone the Miranda rights to Folks as he led him to the back of a patrol car.

As they loaded her into the back of the ambulance, Laura again began to cry.

Chapter 20

Laura spent the night in the hospital. She'd undressed completely, only covered in a hospital gown. She was uncomfortable being naked under the hospital gown. She realized the irony. Normally, she loved being naked. But being naked in a hospital gown reminded her too much of her illegal abortion at an underground clinic in Miami.

When the police officer arrived at the hospital with the clothing from her hotel, she felt relieved.

She quickly got off her hospital bed and put on her panties, setting off alarms as she did so.

A stern-face nurse came running in and gave her a warning about getting out of bed again. She even told Laura to push the button if she needed to use the restroom.

When the nurse turned her back, Laura mouthed to the woman on the bed next to her in the hospital room, "Bitch."

The other woman tried not to laugh, saying she had stitches in her thigh and was recovering from a stab wound. Even laughing hurt, she explained.

Laura tried not to look surprised. She laid back in her bed thinking she was probably in the equivalent of Grady Hospital in Atlanta, where many of the shooting and stabbing victims were sent. Grady was Atlanta's Level 1 Trauma hospital that could treat the most serious and life-threatening injuries.

Sour Grapes

Around ten o'clock, another nurse came in and said the doctor had ordered a sedative for Laura to help her sleep during the night. Laura was scheduled for minor surgery to reset her wrist in the morning.

The nurse reached up to the IV and injected something into the port. Laura almost immediately felt calm and woozy. She was asleep within minutes.

Laura awoke the next morning with dim sunlight coming through the window, unable to remember where she was. Her heart began to race until she remembered she was in the hospital. But that rapid heartbeat set off more alarms and a nurse came in to check on her.

Laura felt sharp pains in her wrist and asked if she could have something for the pain. "I'll have to ask your doctor if we can give you a pain pill."

Laura laid back in her hospital bed and could feel tears begin to well in her eyes. The pain seemed unbearable. Her wrist throbbed.

The nurse returned about an hour later with a small white cup and a pill inside. "This is for your pain. Do you need me to get you some water to take that with?"

Laura nodded. She gulped it down in one swallow.

Around 8 a.m. a hospital breakfast arrived for Laura's hospital mate, but the nurse explained they couldn't feed Laura since she was to have surgery later that afternoon.

Laura frowned. She was so hungry. She hadn't eaten anything since the day before. But then she saw what the other patient was eating.

It looked like bland oatmeal with a piece of dry toast and what she thought was apple sauce. Even though it looked unappetizing, Laura's mouth began to water.

Suddenly she realized she needed to call Kyle Quitman to tell him the events of last night. She tried to reach over to her handbag and nearly pulled her IV out. She could only reach with her left hand, since her right hand was in a splint and bandaged, and, of course, her handbag was on a table to her right.

She fumbled around in her handbag until she found her cellphone. It was hard to try to dial with her left hand. She finally managed to dial Kyle's number, but it went to voicemail.

Laura tried to keep it short and sweet, but she ended up saying the arsonist had tried to kill her and she was now in the hospital and needed surgery on her wrist. Bobby had been arrested for the arson, but she was hoping he'd be released soon since the real arsonist had been arrested. When Laura hung up from the voicemail, she realized she probably sounded like a deranged woman. She hoped he wouldn't take back the offer to hire her.

She put the phone next to her on the bed and dozed off again but awoke to the sound of her cellphone again. It was Bobby.

"Bobby, where are you?"

"I'm still in jail. Why hasn't my attorney called? Did you get the number? I asked you for one favor, Laura! One favor!"

"Well fuck you, Bobby! Walker Folks is the fucking arsonist. He tried to kill me! He doused me with gasoline and tried to burn down the fucking office. He punched me and broke my wrist. I'm in the hospital right now, you asshole! I need surgery!"

Bobby's voice got softer. "You're in the hospital? Walker tried to kill you?"

"He tossed gasoline on me and lit his lighter. Thank God it went out before the gasoline caught, or caught the fumes, or you'd be finding my charred body in the office. In fact, that's what he said he wanted you to find. My charred dead body in the office."

"Oh my God. Laura. I'm so sorry."

Laura could hear Bobby softly crying. Then she began to cry. "I'm sorry I didn't believe you," she croaked.

"Don't cry, baby. Don't cry. I'm supposed to go before the judge this morning and no attorney has called. I'll tell them what you told me. Hopefully they'll release me. What hospital are you in? Queen of the Valley? If they let me go, I'll come get you."

"Ah, yes. I'm at Queen of the Valley Medical Center," Laura said, reading the label off her water cup.

"I don't know what I'd do if I lost you," Bobby said quietly.

Laura said nothing at first, shocked that Bobby expressed what she took to mean deep feelings for her.

"You won't lose me. I'm too much of a bitch to kill. Walker practically said so," she said, trying to laugh. "He pretty much confessed to setting the fire."

"Walker. I would have never suspected him! He's been my right-hand man. Oh shit, I've got to surrender my phone again. Love you."

The line went dead and Laura sat in her hospital bed stunned. Bobby loves her? She certainly cared for him, but love? No. She didn't love any man. She'd made that mistake once and look where it got her. Beaten, raped and pregnant.

No, she'd never love another man. Never. She thought she'd loved Marc Linder, but he made it clear he didn't love her. And now she realized she didn't love him either.

The doctor came around about noon, saying Laura was to go into surgery at 2 p.m. The rest was a blur of preoperative prep. When she came to, she was in recovery. Her mouth was dry, her lips were chapped, and her head ached. So did her wrist, which was in a cast.

When she was wheeled back to her room, the doctor came by to see how she was doing and said he would likely discharge her the next morning. She'd just need some help with everyday chores. Did she have anyone to help?

Laura lied and said she did. A boyfriend that would help her. She didn't want to stay in the hospital for any longer than necessary.

That evening, a bland dinner arrived and Laura was so hungry she gobbled it up. She spent another night in the hospital and was anxious to leave that morning, but by the time all the paperwork was signed it was close to two o'clock.

She was about to call an Uber, praying Greg K. would not be her driver, to take her back to Star 1 to get her car when she got a call from Bobby.

"Bobby! Where are you?"

"On my way to the hospital to see you."

"They just discharged me. I was about to call an Uber."

"Don't. I'll be there in 10 minutes."

"Did the police release you?"

"They sure did. Apologized for the *inconvenience*. I'll definitely be talking to my attorney now to see if I can sue."

"Sue for what?" she asked.

"Some sort of damages for arresting me when I didn't do it. And whose side are you on?" Bobby asked, angry.

"Just come get me," Laura said, not ready to fight with Bobby. "I'm ready to leave this place."

As Laura waited in a wheelchair for Bobby to arrive, Kyle called her back. She repeated what had happened, told him she'd had surgery on her wrist, and said Bobby had been released by the police, since the arsonist had been arrested. She said she wasn't sure when she'd be back in Atlanta, since she was sure the media would be calling about the arson arrest.

He told her to give him an update later that afternoon.

Bobby's truck pulled up at the hospital entrance and Laura smiled, careful of her bandaged lip and wrist, which was in a sling.

She was very happy to see him. Bobby got out of his truck with a big grin, then frowned when he saw her in the wheelchair and the bruise on her face and the steri strips on her bottom lip. When she waved at him, he saw the bright pink cast on her wrist peeking out from the sling.

Bobby's face darkened. "Did Walker do that to you? I'll fucking kill him."

"Shut up. I don't need you being arrested again for making threats," Laura said, allowing Bobby to help her out of the wheelchair and into the passenger side of his truck.

"What happened?" they asked at the same time.

"You first," Laura said.

"I went before the judge. The police said they arrested Walker on suspicion of arson, they said they were sorry for the inconvenience and they released me. Now you."

"I went to the winery and found Walker, but he said he didn't have the key. He said you did. But I didn't believe him. Something was off about his story. I went back to my hotel and called a locksmith to come out to open the office. Thank God! Eric saved me!"

"Who's Eric? The locksmith?"

"Yes. I got to the office yesterday before Eric was supposed to show up and the office door was open. I went in and Walker was there with a gas can. He threw gas on me and then on the desk and floor. He tried to light me on fire."

Bobby shuddered as he drove. "Oh my God. How did you get the busted lip and hurt wrist?"

"He hit me and then shoved me on the floor. I didn't realize I'd broken it until later. Then he said 'Die, bitch' and lit his lighter. It was a miracle it went out and didn't ignite the fumes. They were pretty bad. The fumes were making me dizzy."

Bobby pulled into the winery and parked in front of the office, which had crime tape across the door. He reached over and tried to hold Laura close, but it was an awkward hug.

He went around to the passenger door and helped her out of the truck and held her close. "I'll never forgive him for what he did to you," he whispered.

"I don't think you'll have to worry about him. He kind of confessed in front of the police. Said something about needing more money."

"Did he say why he did it? Did he say why he tried to burn the winery and the office? He worked here."

"He didn't say really. Just said he needed more money than he made at the winery. Maybe he told the police more by now, but I don't."

They walked arm in arm toward Bobby's house. "Stay tonight?" he whispered in her hair.

Laura turned to face him. "Yes. I want to stay with you tonight. I want to feel safe."

"You'll be safe with me."

Laura was correct when she told Kyle the media would be calling about the arson arrest. Her phone blew up with call after call. She was reluctant to have the media out to the winery for a press release or a video interview given her fat lip, bruised face and right arm in a sling. She didn't want to have to explain what had happened to her personally.

She knew the media wouldn't call after the start of the evening news, so she held them off with statements over the phone, keeping them off the property and gave no in-person interviews.

Laura then called Kyle with a final wrap up and fell into Bobby's arms on the couch. He had started a fire in the fireplace and opened a bottle of the Cabernet reserve. She awkwardly held the wine glass in her left hand.

"If we have dinner tonight, you are going to have to cut up my meat," Laura quipped, holding up her bright pink cast.

"I'll spoon feed you if I have to," he smiled back.

They ended up ordering pizza for dinner. "Kind of a waste of good wine with this pizza, right?" Laura asked.

"I think this will pair very well with it," he replied, holding up his glass to the light, before taking a big bite of the sausage, mushroom and pepperoni pizza. "Do I need to cut up your pizza?"

"I think I can manage," she said before rolling up the slice and taking a bite. But she was finding it more difficult to use her left hand. Many times she reached for her wine glass with her right hand, only to have to stop and then use her left hand. Laura had taken off the sling to eat. She often held her right wrist and rubbed it.

Bobby noticed and asked, "Does it hurt?"

"Yes. The skin under the cast really itches. I don't know how I'm going to carry my bags back to Atlanta, especially with the sling on," she said.

Bobby looked up with alarm. "You're going back? When?"

"Kyle gave me a week. He'll probably extend it since I'm injured. I certainly do not want to get on an airplane looking like a victim of domestic violence. And I doubt he'll send his private jet back just for me. That was a sweet ride out here, though."

"I didn't realize you were leaving so soon."

"I guess I'll have to come back to testify, so I won't be gone forever. I would like to know what they've charged Walker with. I'm surprised they haven't contacted you. I'm sure you'll have to testify, too. You knew that receipt wasn't right. He must have planted it."

Bobby took another bite of his pizza and chewed slowly, thinking. "I guess you are right. I will have to testify if they've charged him. Maybe he needs a bond hearing like they were going to do for me. That will probably be tomorrow, I guess. I just can't believe it was Walker! I would never have suspected him."

"Can you think of anything that might have upset him?"

"I remember he wasn't too happy when I sold my share of the winery to Quitman. I think he was afraid he'd lose his job. He's worked here for 10 years at least. But when Quitman said not to change anything — any of the personnel — I thought he was okay with that."

"Did his benefits change or anything? His pay?"

"Quitman talked about everyone moving over to his benefit plan. Seems decent enough, but I don't have a wife and kids like Walker does. It's just me."

"No kids? I know you said you were divorced, but you didn't have children?"

"Nope. That's kind of why we divorced."

"Oh."

"No kids for you?" Bobby asked.

Laura's face darkened for a slight second, then she said, "No. Never married. No kids."

"You don't have to get married to have kids, you know."

"Do I look like I have a single maternal bone in my body?"

Bobby laughed wryly. "No, I don't suppose you do. I want to ask you something. Will you stay with me? I mean, be my publicist? You know, keep up the website, work the events. An event planner maybe."

Laura was stunned. She had no idea Bobby wanted her to stay permanently.

"Bobby, I can't. I can't just pull up roots and stay here. Besides, Kyle offered me a permanent job out in Atlanta."

Bobby's face fell. "But I love you. I don't want to lose you."

"I'm sorry, Bobby. I had no idea you felt that way."

"You're saying you won't stay?"

"No. I assumed you knew that. I am only here temporarily."

"Am I just temporary? A temporary plaything? A boy toy?" Bobby shouted, jumping up from the table. He slammed his hands down on the table, making Laura jump. "God, Laura I told you I love you and you feel nothing! Nothing!"

"I don't feel nothing for you, Bobby. I just don't love you," Laura said, trying to keep her voice low and controlled. "And it's time for me to go home."

"You really know how to hurt a guy, don't you?" Bobby shot back.

"Why? Because I'm not in love with you? You know as well as I do this was just temporary."

"Temporary? I'm asking you to stay, Laura. Come live with me and help me build this winery back. I can do it with you. I know I can."

Laura could see he was hurt. She was sorry they were having another fight, but she couldn't stay in Napa. She didn't want to stay in Napa. She wanted her life back. Her life in Atlanta.

"Bobby. I don't want to fight with you. I'm sorry I don't feel the same way you do. Maybe I should go."

Laura tried to get up from the table but found it hard to leverage herself with just one hand.

"No, don't go," he said, quickly walking over to stop her. "I would like you to stay tonight. You said you would feel safer here with me. Please stay. I won't talk any more about us being together tonight."

"Maybe I should go. I only have these clothes. I don't have any of my things. The police went to my hotel and brought me these clothes to the hospital."

"Where are your other clothes?"

"They had gasoline all over them. They took them as evidence. Bagged them up. I was afraid they were going to take my boots too. I talked them out of it."

Bobby smiled wanly. "Your boots? You like them now, don't you?"

"I like them a lot. I like the wise man who told me to buy a pair."

Two weeks later, at the end of June, Bobby helped Laura with her bags at the San Francisco Airport. She checked her bags and stood outside security with Bobby.

"I wish you weren't going," he said.

"I know, but I must. I'll see you when the trial starts."

"If it starts. Walker could take a plea deal."

"He'd be smart to do that," she said. "I see the news reports that he's saying he did it because of gambling debts. But he hasn't said who was paying him to do it."

"No, he hasn't. I'd really like to know to paid him. I'd like to know who I'm up against."

"Maybe he'll confess all."

"I hope he doesn't because I want to see you again. I love you, Laura. I know you don't feel the same way, but…"

"I care deeply for you, Bobby, and I wish you all the best with the winery. I'll be administering the website, at least for now. Lee sent over the file for the video of the winery. It looks great. We've got all those photos of the models. I think Star 1 is going to be a star."

Bobby held Laura in a tight hug. "I wish you weren't going."

Laura looked into his sad eyes, then kissed him deeply. "I've got to go," she said, putting her left hand on his chest and gently pushing him away. "I don't want to miss my flight. I'll call you when I get home."

She turned to go through the security checkpoint and didn't look back. Laura did not want Bobby to see the relief on her face as she left him. Laura broke out into a wide smile as she strode toward her departure gate.

Made in the USA
Columbia, SC
04 August 2024

39951153R00119